MIDNIGHT TRAIN

Angela was famous at seventeen as a hotpants-wearing girl in her own adventure TV show. Now, at forty-five, her marriage has fallen apart, and she daren't so much as look at those tiny hotpants. Mike is a vicar with a secret past, struggling to deal with the death of his wife and the stress of his job. Both are looking to escape their troubles as they board the Midnight Train to Cariastan, but neither can know it will be a journey that threatens their very lives . . .

Books by Sally Quilford
in the Linford Romance Library:

THE SECRET OF HELENA'S BAY
BELLA'S VINEYARD
A COLLECTOR OF HEARTS
MY TRUE COMPANION
AN IMITATION OF LOVE
SUNLIT SECRETS
MISTLETOE MYSTERY
OUR DAY WILL COME
BONFIRE MEMORIES

SALLY QUILFORD

MIDNIGHT TRAIN

Complete and Unabridged

LINFORD
Leicester

First published in Great Britain in 2013

First Linford Edition
published 2014

A catalogue record for this book is available
from the British Library.

ISBN 978–1–4448–1936–6

R

1

'Come on, Angela. Put on the gold hot pants once more, just for old time's sake.'

'You're kidding, Ken,' said Angela Cunningham. She grimaced at the webcam. On her laptop screen, Ken's well-fed jowls seemed even bigger than normal. 'The last time I wore those hot pants I was seventeen years old, and, if I may say so myself, had a great bum. Now I'm forty-five, and for some reason I need scaffolding to stop my backside from dragging behind me as I walk.'

'Rubbish. You looked great in those jodhpurs on that drama you were in last week.'

'Oh, that . . . ' Angela scoffed. 'I couldn't have possibly been the murderer, as the false leg they found under the seat in the parlour was completely the wrong size for me.'

'You're saying the murderer was someone else with a false leg.'

'Must have been.'

'Did you tell the writer that?'

'Oh yes, Ken, I'm going to tell the best crime dramatist in Britain how to write her screenplays. Besides it was a cock up in the props department. Did you see that Pina Colada my character was supposed to be drinking? I've never seen one so overdressed. Nearly had my eye out with an umbrella! In fact, if it had been a false eye under the seat, it would probably have been the wrong colour.'

'Anyway,' said Ken, sighing. 'Back to the subject in hand. *Pandora's Vox* still sells loads on DVD, Angie.'

Oh no, thought Angela. When Ken started to call her Angie, she knew he was going in for the big schmooze. It meant there was a lot of money behind it for him. She ought to cut him off now, whilst she still had all the gold fillings in her teeth.

'And,' said Ken, warming to his theme, 'the fans still turn up in droves at the conventions.'

'Ken, I'm too old to play that role now. I'm not knocking Pandora. She's been good to me. In fact I still make more from her, in royalties and appearance fees, than I do from any of my other acting roles. She bought this house.' Angela spread her hands to take in the scene behind her. She was sitting in the large live-in kitchen of her Victorian villa in London. Through the concertina windows that covered one wall she could see boats idling along the Thames, which ran across the bottom of her garden. She loved the house and everything in it. 'But I'd be a laughing stock if I were to put on those hot pants again.'

'David Tennant is interested . . . '

'He is?' Ken almost piqued Angela's interest. Working with David Tennant would be wonderful. But she was also used to the tricks her agent used to get her to do things she did not want to do.

3

'I bet he isn't. I bet he doesn't even know about it.'

'Well, I put the idea to his agent, who's going to get back to me.'

'Oh yeah . . . ' Angela reached forward and put her finger on the keyboard, ready to delete Ken's face from view.

'Don't cut me off, Angela.'

'Bye, Ken.'

'I'll call you tomorrow when you're not so . . . menopausal,' said Ken, savagely.

'I love you too, Ken. Bye.'

Angela sighed impatiently. Why did dealing with her agent always have to be so fraught with difficulty? He was supposed to work for her, and get a commission for his pains, but it did not always feel that way. In many ways, she was afraid of Ken. He was very powerful in the entertainment industry and if he decided to drop her, she would struggle to find another agent. But that did not mean she was willing to be bullied into reprising the role that had made her famous.

She always hated actors who were embarrassed by the roles that had given them their big break, which was why she refused to be ashamed of *Pandora's Vox*. The adventures of a hot pant wearing teenage girl who could get into other worlds via her television screen had caught the imagination of a generation. Looking back at the show and with all the CGI available nowadays, the wonky sets and shaky graphics of *Pandora's Vox* were sometimes laughable. But the fans still loved it. They spent hours on Internet message boards going over every word Pandora had ever said, every relationship she had ever had, to find some meaning that, as far as Angela knew, had never been there.

But being proud of the role that made her famous and trying to relive the time when she was younger, slimmer and prettier were two different things. She risked becoming a laughing stock. Angela had long since resigned herself to becoming older and therefore playing either ageing *femme fatales* or the mother of the heroine in British television dramas. There were few other roles for women of her age.

She made herself a cup of coffee and wandered around the house, where the memorabilia of her career was on show in several glass cases. In one case in the hallway, there was a broken Union Jack umbrella, which Pandora had used to fight off Hitler. In another case, in the sitting room, was a strange black cube that it took Angela a moment to recall. Oh yes, it had held the secrets of the universe. But Pandora had decided not to look, because she realised that it was not a good idea to know everything. Besides, being called Pandora had tipped the character off to the inherent problems of opening up any box. Angela opened the case and picked it up, bouncing it in her hand. She very much doubted that the secrets of the universe would be encased in balsa wood, but who knew? She wished it would give her the answers that she was seeking.

As for the infamous hot pants, they were hidden under some *Pandora's Vox* annuals, simply because Angela could not bear to look at them anymore. Visitors always asked to see them, but she always claimed they had been lost. Had she ever fit into those tiny things? Because God forbid that the hot pants would not fit one week, or would have to be swapped for a larger pair. They brought back unhappier memories.

The one enduring memory she had from those days was always being hungry, then of not bothering to eat at all just in case an extra inch on her bum meant she would lose her role to a younger, slimmer actress. As it was, it was all over by the time she was twenty-one. At least the role was over. The effects of all the pressures put on her by the wardrobe department lasted for a long time afterwards.

She sighed and closed the case. She wished Ken had not contacted her. Not today, of all days. On the coffee table in the sitting room was a gossip magazine. And on the cover was the headline, *Angus and Chloe Peterson's Baby Joy*.

The cover showed a middle aged, but still very handsome A-list actor, with his pretty young wife, who was famous for being a contestant on a reality show. She was carrying a small dog in her handbag, though it was hard to tell one from the other. Maybe, thought Angela, it was just a handbag and some bright designer had realised that z-list celebrities needed handbags that looked like pooches to save all that having to go walkies and clean up doggy mess. Chloe's pneumatic lips almost popped out from the magazine cover, whilst her tummy was remarkably flat. Of course, it did not do to show one's pregnancy in this day and age for fear of being labelled fat. Angela felt a little bit sorry for Chloe Peterson. But mostly she felt as if she had been stabbed in the heart.

She slumped on the sofa, and browsed through the magazine, even though she had read the story more than once already. It spoke of Angus Peterson's longing for children, but how, until now he had been denied that joy. A journalist had telephoned Angela only a couple of days earlier to ask her for a quote. According to the report, Angela had said 'icily' 'I'm very happy for them.' Well, perhaps she had said it icily, but that was mostly because the journalist spent the first half of the conversation reminding Angela of her inability to have children.

She threw the magazine down in tears of frustration and picked up a newspaper, idly reading the contents, trying to think of anything but the story in the gossip mag. One of the articles was an extended advert for the Midnight Train from Nice to Cariastan. It included the history of Cariastan, which Angela was forced to admit she had never heard of until picking up the paper. That was alluded to by the journalist, who called Cariastan Eastern Europe's best kept secret. Overlooking the Black Sea, Cariastan was a tiny, but extremely pretty country that was made up of Russians, Greeks, Italians, Turks and Romanians. Its name meant The Place of the Heart. It was also becoming known, due to the amount of rich people who were drawn to Cariastan's golden beaches and fine hotels, as the Eastern Monaco.

The mixture of peoples, and the fact that the country had once been part of the Ottoman Empire, had left Cariastan's capital city, also called Cariastan, with stunning architecture, which included Moorish villas, domed mosques, Jewish temples, whitewashed Greek Orthodox churches, and tall cathedrals. As Cariastan did not have its own tongue, the most commonly used language was English.

The previous king, who fell in love with and married a commoner, had come to the throne before World War Two. He had been something of a republican, and after the war, he had given his country back to the people.

Unfortunately political infighting led to the Soviet Union marching into Cariastan in the nineteen-sixties on a day known to the people as Tyrannical Tuesday.

The country had spent over forty years under communist rule, but the people had recently voted to return to a monarchy in the hopes of reliving former glories and encouraging tourism. Prince Henri, the great-grandson of the previous king, was due to be crowned very soon and the whole country was celebrating. The advertisement spoke of an exciting journey in luxurious surroundings, with fine dining and, Angela guessed, a lot of time out of mobile phone and Internet range. The train would travel for over thirty hours, arriving in Cariastan at midnight on the eve of the coronation.

Impulsively Angela picked up the phone and dialled the number. Five minutes later she had booked a double cabin on the train that left Nice the very next night. She contacted an airline and booked a last minute flight to Nice. Then she telephoned her mum and dad to let them know she would be gone for a while.

'I understand, darling,' Meredith Cunningham said. 'Daddy and I just saw the magazine. Not that we buy it. We were at the newsagents. But you could have come to us.' There was only a hint of reproach in Meredith's voice.

'I know, mum, but I need to get away from Britain for a bit, that's all.'

'Please come and see us when you get back. So we know you're alright.'

'I will, mum. Give dad my love.'

Angela put the phone down, half afraid that Meredith would talk her into going to Midchester. She loved her parents to bits, and as the baby of the family, she had always been cossetted. But she knew that Meredith would fuss too much, and she was afraid that if that happened, she really would break down.

She would simply get away from it all. The hot pants she could no longer fit into, the 'baby joy' and her own failure as a woman writ large for everyone to see on the cover of a glossy magazine.

★ ★ ★

Mike Fairfax knew he had to get away. Every day of his life was filled with people making demands upon his time. He could not complain. After all, he had signed up for it. But this latest tragedy in the village of Stony End had left everyone reeling and for once the normally certain Mike Fairfax had struggled to find the right thing to say. Then when he did speak out, he said all the wrong things.

If anyone was due time off, it must be him. He had continued working through the death of his wife, through the time the village was flooded in a bad storm and then through the disappearance of a young child. The worst of it was that Mike had counselled the parents, and they had clung to him, letting him absorb their pain like a sponge. When the child was found he had exploded in a rage that many said must have been lying dormant for years.

He shook his head. He could not think about it anymore. Maybe it was time for him to be selfish. One of the villagers had just come back from a trip across Europe and mentioned the Midnight Train from Nice to Cariastan. He had always wanted to go on a trip like that. In fact, he and his wife, Julia, had discussed it. It was always one of those things they were going to do someday. Unfortunately before some-day arrived, Julia was taken from him.

Mike booked the trip online, not bothering to read the terms and conditions. He had made up his mind to go and he did not much care how many extras he had to pay for, as long as he got away.

He telephoned his son to let him know.

'Hi dad, how are you?' Jamie

sounded wary, as did everyone who spoke to Mike nowadays. His meltdown had been very public, after all.

'I'm fine, son. I just wanted you to know I'm going away for a few days.'

'That's great, dad. It's just what you need. You could come to me if you wanted. Cheap beer in the student bar and all that.'

'Sounds good, but I'm taking a train from Nice to Cariastan. Then I'll spend a few days there sightseeing and find another way home. I could be gone a while.'

'Wow, that's fantastic. Really, dad. It's something you should do. I wish I could go with you, but with my finals coming up, I can't manage the time away.' Jamie was in his last year at vet school. Michael wanted to point out that Jamie only needed the barest pass to get through with flying colours, but his son had always been conscientious, especially when it came to veterinary science.

'No, it's alright, son. I need to be

alone for a while. Do you mind?'

'Nah, of course not. It's just it seems to me you're always alone, dad. I worry about you.'

'The feeling is mutual.'

'Hey, who knows, perhaps you'll meet some Russian princess and fall in love.'

'I think they got rid of all the Russian princesses during the revolution, Jamie. And that was a long time before Russia took over Cariastan. But history never was your strong point, was it?' There was no malice in Mike's words. His son knew he was proud of him. From childhood, Jamie had spent all his free time helping out at the various farms and stables around Stony End.

'Well, you know what I mean. Have a good time, Dad. Give me a call when you get back home and we'll get together.'

'I'd like that. See you soon, son.'

He ran upstairs to pack, taking off his dog-collar and grey shirt as he did so. He shoved both into a drawer and slammed it shut.

As Mike changed, he had a sudden feeling of a cold hand on his spine. His grandmother used to call it a 'Sugar plum fairy dancing on one's grave'. He fought the urge to ring Jamie again, feeling, unaccountably that it might be the last time he ever spoke to his son . . .

★   ★   ★

'I really think we should go with him, Harry,' said Liberty Cathcart, as she arranged the flowers for the church. They only lived a few doors away, so she liked to do them and take them over all ready. That way the other ladies in the friends of the church group would never see just how long it took her to get it right.

'He asked us to feed his cat,' said Harry Cathcart, looking up from his newspaper. 'If we don't do that, who will?'

'Oh, his cleaner, Polly, will do that anyway.'

'He said she has enough to do cleaning up after him. And I don't think she gets on with his cat.'

'No, Harry, I've made up my mind. I promised poor dear Julia I would look after him.'

'Julia Fairfax died only three weeks after we moved to Stony End.'

'Well, I promised her in prayer that we would, because Mike has always been so good to us. Who knows what might happen to him if he heads off to Europe alone? Especially after . . . ' She lowered her voice. 'You know what.'

'He was justifiably angry about something,' said Harry.

'Well, yes, I agree. But even so a vicar isn't supposed to go so . . . well mad. It makes people distrust him. He's in a vulnerable state of mind, Harry. He should not be alone.'

'Liberty, we are not going to follow Reverend Fairfax abroad. Liberty?'

★ ★ ★

The station in Nice was a hub of activity as the train unloaded passengers and cargo, and started to load all that would be needed for the two day trip to Cariastan. Trolleys loaded with cutlery; fresh food for the main restaurant car; sandwiches and other snacks for the buffet car; enough alcohol and soft drinks to quench every thirst; clean bedding and everything else needed to ensure that everyone taking the journey would have everything they required.

The train, with its white and gold livery — the colours of the Cariastan Royal Family — would also have to be refuelled. As soon as everyone was off the train, the two drivers, who split the gruelling journey between them, had detached the engine from the carriages and moved into a siding, where attendants filled it up with diesel.

'Come on, Will,' said Cal, looking back for his friend, as he pushed a trolley up to the doors of the kitchen carriage. 'What you daydreaming about? The new *Resident Evil* film?'

The words chalk and cheese immediately came to mind with Will and Cal. Though both around eighteen, working their gap year, they were complete opposites. Cal was pale, grey-eyed, with long blond hair, tied back in a ponytail. He had the physique of an Olympic athlete, but claimed never to exercise, preferring people to believe it was natural.

Will was of mixed race, with thick dark curls, cut close to his head, and startling blue eyes that made girls look at him and look again. He was bigger built than Cal, with broad shoulders and a natural muscle tone that took his friend ages to achieve in the gym.

'Actually, mate,' said Will, pushing his own trolley further back, towards the carriages. 'I was thinking about an old film I watched on telly in the hotel last night. It was called *The Colossus of New York* and it had this robot. Well the robot had a man's brain in it and ... Well I'm not sure what happened because it was dubbed in French.'

'Boring,' said Cal, cutting in. 'Your French ought to be getting better now, the time we've worked on this train.'

'I'm not bad at French,' said Will. 'I just can't understand it if it's spoken too fast, that's all.' Will stopped a moment and looked across the station towards the diesel pumps. 'Hey, Cal, look over there. Who are those blokes? I don't remember seeing them on the train.'

'They take on new staff all the time,' said Cal, sounding bored.

'Are you two planning to work today?' asked Monsieur Ambroise, sticking his head out of one of the carriage windows. 'Or are you just going to talk about your films, Monsieur Guillaume?' The head porter glared at Will, but barely glanced at Cal.

'Sorry, Monsieur,' said Will, whose full name was William Carmichael. He kind of liked the way Ambroise said his name. It made it sound more interesting. 'I just wondered what those men were doing over near the engine.'

'They are filling it with diesel, I imagine,' said Ambroise. 'Now, come.' He clapped his hands together briskly. 'We have to get ready for the passengers.' His voice dropped a little and he said indifferently, 'You too, Cal.' He pronounced it 'Coll'.

Will was beginning to wonder if Monsieur Ambroise was racist. He always received the sharp end of Ambroise's tongue, whereas Cal got away with all sorts. Cal had once used one of the cabins for a tryst with a girlfriend. Ambroise had merely shrugged it off. Will felt sure he would not get away with doing the same.

Mind you, thought Will miserably, when your father runs one of the biggest banks in the world, you can probably do whatever you want. It would not matter to Cal if he were sacked. When you're a kid who has been brought up in a series of foster homes, you had to play by the rules, especially if you needed to start saving to pay off your university fees.

Never down for long, Will shrugged it off, and got on with his work. He quite liked working on the Cariastan train. There were always interesting people to meet. But as he loaded boxes onto the train he looked across at the engine again. As he did so, he felt sure that the sun suddenly went behind a cloud. He shivered, and tightened up his tunic, feeling an icy hand tickle his spine. But when he looked up, the sun was still shining high above him, and there was not a cloud to be seen.

★   ★   ★

The two strange men next to the engine went around to the back, where one of the drivers was filling the tank.

From that angle, they could not be seen from the station or by the nosy black boy who had been watching them. The driver would be found in one of the sheds the next day with a slashed throat, but just for then one of the men knocked him out cold and left him on the ground, whilst the other man did the same to the other driver, who would also be found dead when it was too late to do anything.

One man continued to fill the tank, whilst the other set up the device under the floor of the engine cab. His hands shook as he did so. One wrong move and the device would go off too soon. Nice was not the target, as he had been told a dozen times by the man they called 'The Handler'. Not that they had ever met him. He made sure that the people involved in the plan only knew *what* they needed to know and *who* they needed to know.

At the allotted time, the train moved back onto the main track and re-attached to the carriages. Such was the chaos and confusion as everyone got onto the train and found their sleeping compartments, no one noticed that the engine driver and his mate were men who had never been seen on that railroad before.

When the all-clear was sounded, the Midnight Train started to move along the tracks, building up speed as it left Nice behind. In just over 24 hours, the passengers would not be all that was delivered to the capital of Cariastan. What they did not know, and would not know until it was too late, was that it was intended to be a one way trip.

2

Angela lugged her case along the corridor, looking for her cabin number. She had to get past a young mum, whose cute little blond son was playing with a dinosaur. The young woman, who was holding a half-eaten apple, was obviously trying to keep him occupied. Food had not worked, so dinosaurs were clearly the next best thing. They looked tired, as if they had been travelling for some time.

The child roared and waved the dinosaur at Angela as she passed by. She turned and said 'Ra ra,' in a growly voice, laughing as she did so. She was rewarded with a cheeky grin from the little boy. When he made to follow her, thinking he had found a playmate, his mum had to grab him.

'No, Solomon, no. Stay here. Sorry,' she said, curtly.

'Oh it's no problem at all. He's adorable.'

'You think?' the girl said, wryly. It seemed that the young mum was too tired to love him at that particular moment. Angela felt certain it was momentary, and that really the mother adored the little boy.

He roared at Angela again, and she spent a few moments roaring back at him, before sensing that the mother was getting annoyed. 'Sorry,' Angela said. 'I just can't resist cute kids.'

The woman raised a quizzical eyebrow. 'Really? I find I can resist them very easily.'

Angela felt awkward then, then chastised herself. She, more than anyone, should understand that one should not judge women by their ability to be maternal. Even so, she felt sorry for the little boy with a mother who could obviously take him or leave him. She hoped he had a daddy to make up for the lack of love. Or maybe the girl really was too tired from travelling and

Angela was being unfair. She smiled uncertainly at the woman and went on her way.

She finally found her cabin in a carriage further along, as the moving train jostled her from side to side. She pushed the door open and saw a tall fair-haired man, who had his suitcase on the seat. She did not know what to say to begin with. As if sensing her presence he turned around and asked 'Can I help you?'

'Well yes, erm . . . I think there's been some mistake. This is my cabin. See? Fifteen A.' She held out the ticket she had printed at home. 'It says it on here. Fifteen A. So this is my cabin.'

'No, this is definitely my cabin. Look . . . ' He took his own ticket out of his pocket. 'Oh, it says Fifteen B.'

'Oh don't worry, it's an easy mistake. You're probably just next door.'

The man went out into the corridor, having to squeeze past Angela as he did so. He smelled of Sandalwood soap, and was rather hunky in a very

English public school type of way. He was tall with broad shoulders under a black crew neck sweater and a tweed jacket. He looked to be the professor type. His hair was sun-kissed blond, his eyes were ice-blue, and his face had a fine smattering of freckles that were extremely appealing. Very Charles Dance, thought Angela.

The strange man looked at the doors on the cabins either side of them, and then at the door on the cabin he and Angela were debating.

'I think we've both made a mistake,' he said. 'This door has plaques saying 'Fifteen A and Fifteen B'. I've a dreadful feeling it means the bunks. Top and bottom. A and B.'

'No, it can't be,' said Angela. 'I specifically booked a double en suite cabin to be alone and to have more space.' She had hoped she could keep the top bunk made up as a bed, and then just use the bottom bunk for daytime lounging.

He raised an eyebrow. 'Yes, I had the

same idea. I'll go and find a porter. I'm sure we can sort this out.'

A few moments later, the man returned with a young porter. He was a good looking black guy, with a ready smile. His name badge said William.

'I'm sorry sir and madam,' Will said in a South London accent, 'but the double cabins aren't gender specific.'

'What exactly does that mean?' asked Angela.

'It means that we can't guarantee you won't be sharing with someone of the opposite sex.'

'But I booked this cabin to myself,' she argued.

'As did I,' said the tall fair-haired man.

'No, you booked the individual bunks,' said Will. 'It does explain on the website.'

'I don't remember reading that,' said Angela. In truth she had been in such a hurry to leave Britain, she had not bothered looking at the terms and conditions.

'No, I don't remember seeing it,' said the tall man. Angela briefly wondered if he were running away from something too. 'Look erm . . . William.' He put his hand in his pocket and took out his wallet. 'I'm sure we can sort this out. If you could find me another cabin, I'll be happy to pay the extra.'

'I'm sorry, sir,' said Will. 'But there are no other cabins. We're booked up.'

'Oh . . . ' said Angela, crestfallen. 'Well, couldn't you find a couple — a man and a woman — who might be willing to let one of us swap?'

'I could try, madam.'

'Good lad. There'll be a tip in it from both of us if you do,' she said with a smile.

The porter went off in the other direction, and started knocking on doors.

'I'm sure it will be sorted out,' said Angela.

'Oh yes, I'm sure. I'm Mike Fairfax, by the way. If we're going to nearly share a cabin, I feel we should know each other's names.'

'Angela Cunningham.' She held out her hand. 'It was nice almost knowing you, Mike . . . I mean in the social sense,' she said, blushing. 'Not in the Biblical sense. And now I'm waffling because I'm embarrassed.' And rather attracted to you, she thought silently.

'I knew what you meant.'

'Thank goodness, because half the time I don't know what comes out of my mouth.'

'It's a very attractive mouth.'

Was he flirting with her? She did believe he was! 'Thank you.' Angela sat down on the seat in the cabin, convinced she would be staying there. He had already proved himself a gentleman by offering to take another carriage. No doubt he would insist on moving when they were able to swap. 'What brings you on this journey?'

'Excitement and a chance to see new faces. You?'

'Much the same, along with a need to get out of Britain for a while.'

'I'm sorry,' said Mike. 'I promise this isn't a line, but I feel that I know your face from somewhere.' He sat down next to her, as if they had been friends forever. It was not an unwelcome feeling to have him so close.

'I'm an actress,' said Angela. She went into corny voiceover mode. 'You may remember me from *Midsomer Murders*, *Murder She Wrote*, dozens of other dramas with murder in the title, and an advert for chicken stock cubes, in which I would have liked to murder the foul-mouthed celebrity chef who was starring alongside me.'

Mike laughed. 'Angela Cunningham. How stupid of me not to realise. I know you now. You're surely leaving out the best part of your career.'

'Oh no,' said Angela, laughing. 'Please don't say it. That's one of the things I'm escaping from.'

'*Pandora's Vox*? It was every young nerd's favourite show at one time. I know because I was that nerd.'

'If you mention the hot pants, I may

have to throw you off the train. My agent wants me to don them again.'

'I'm sure half the men in Britain wouldn't mind.'

'Oh believe me,' said Angela. 'They would! Some things are better left in the past, don't you think?'

'Well, if your agent gets up a petition, I must warn you that I will sign it.'

'So,' said Angela. 'What do you do, nerd?'

'At the moment I don't do anything. I'm taking a break. I worked in . . . counselling.'

Angela could not help but notice the pause before he said counselling. She sensed immediately that he had lied to her. 'Strange, I thought you were going to say computers.'

'I did, for a while, in a manner of speaking, when I was in the army. Then I changed directions.'

'And became a counsellor?'

'Yes.'

Before they could continue their conversation, Will returned. 'I'm sorry,

34

sir and madam, I really tried, but there's no chance of changing cabins tonight. Everyone wants to stay put. Tomorrow, some people get off in Innsbruck, but I don't know yet if all the cabins will be used. Sometimes people just don't turn up. So you'll have to share for tonight. Unless one of you would like to sit up in the restaurant car.'

'Yes, I could do that,' said Mike.

'No,' Angela protested, even though she was not sure if she could trust herself with this gorgeous man. And yet, she knew instinctively that he would behave, even if she could not. There was something about him that engendered trust. She had only ever known one man who had that effect on people; her father. 'I wouldn't dream of you having to sit up all night, Mike. We're both sensible, mature adults. I'm sure we can manage to share a cabin for one night without any problems.'

'Very well, then that's settled,' said

Mike. 'Thank you, Angela. And thank you, William.'

'Most people call me Will, sir.'

'Thanks Will. Oh, I don't suppose you've got any films for the DVD player, have you?' She pointed to the one on the wall. 'I forgot to pack any.'

'I've got loads,' said Will. 'Last night I was watching the Colossus of New York. You could borrow that if you wanted to.'

'Oh I love that film,' said Angela. 'Mind you, when I was little it creeped me out. My dad had to tell me that at the end the robot gets up and they all go out for fish and chips.'

Mike laughed. 'That's rather sweet of him.'

'Well, he's a vicar,' said Angela. 'He doesn't like to think of anyone being afraid, least of all his youngest daughter.'

She did not know if she imagined it, but Mike seemed to stiffen beside her. But his voice was amicable when he said to Will, 'Could Miss Cunningham and I have some drinks, Will? What are you having, Angela? It's my tab.'

'Angela . . . ' said Will slowly. Then the light began to dawn on his face. 'Angela Cunningham. *Pandora's Vox* Angela Cunningham? I knew I'd seen you before. I've got the entire series on DVD!'

'You too, eh, Will?' said Mike, with a wicked grin.

'If anyone mentions gold hot pants, I may have to scream,' said Angela, wryly. Yet there was something about being with Mike that made it all seem silly and funny, even if she was more than twenty years older and could no longer fit into the hot pants.

'I've always wanted to ask,' said Will, 'whether the final episode, where Pandora is trapped in the television was a metaphor for lost youth.'

'Well,' said Angela, her lips curling into a wicked smile. She had heard many such theories before. 'It was either that or just a cliff-hanger that would have been resolved if they hadn't cancelled the series.'

'Oh,' said Will. He looked so disappointed that Angela felt awful for having teased him.

'But I think you're right,' she said. 'It was a metaphor for lost youth, and the way the media swallows us all up in the end.'

'Brilliant,' said Will, giving her the thumbs up. 'Wait till I tell them on the *Pandora's Vox* forum that I heard that from a reliable source!'

'That was naughty,' said Mike, as Will went off down the corridor to fetch the drinks they had ordered.

'I didn't want to disappoint him. He's a sweetheart.'

'Have I got a rival?'

'Well he is gorgeous too. But also young enough to be my . . . nephew.'

'No, just your younger brother, I'm sure. I'm starving, Angela. How about you?'

'Yes, I am a bit hungry.'

'What do you fancy? Fine dining or a sandwich in the buffet car?'

'I had my heart set on a nice juicy steak.'

'The main restaurant it is then.'

After an hour, two delicious steaks with chips, and several small bottles of spirits later, Angela and Mike were getting on like a house on fire in the restaurant car. It was decked out in the same livery as the rest of the train, and very fine indeed. The staff spoke English, Arabic, Greek and Russian, which meant that the carriage was filled with the soft babble of different languages and the clink clink of cutlery. One porter, who, according to his name badge was called Ambroise, also spoke French.

He seemed to be in charge and kept looking disapprovingly at a young blond porter who spent rather too much time chatting up the single women in the restaurant instead of getting on with his job. The women did not seem to mind and Angela hazarded a guess that he would be tipped well. She wondered where Will was. They had not seen him since he brought them their drinks.

Angela mused that if the train had been on a film set, then all the women would have been wearing evening dresses, and all the men would be in tuxedos. Someone would be at the bar shaking up cocktails. As it was, people were dressed casually in jeans, jogging pants and fleece sweaters. Admittedly most of those sweaters and jogging pants had the names of high end designers, but there was still a very informal air to the proceedings. Angela and Mike both wore jeans, but Angela had changed into a sparkly top, thinking she ought to make some effort. Whether for dinner or for Mike, she would not admit to herself.

One guy, who had a lion's mane of blond hair, was dressed in black leather trousers and waistcoat, under which he wore a long sleeved tee shirt that was decorated with a skull and crossbones. Angela felt sure she knew him from somewhere, but could not place him.

He was looking around as if seeking someone out. His eyes kept going to the young man who was chatting up the girls.

Over dinner, Angela learned that Mike was fifty years old and had a son who was in his final year at vet school.

'What do you plan to do in Cariastan?' she asked, and then worried that he might think she would try to latch onto him when they got there.

'Sightseeing, the usual. You?'

'Oh I want to swim in the Black Sea. The beaches look wonderful.'

'Sadly I can't swim.'

'What? You can't swim? Really?'

'Really. I know it's pathetic, at my age. But I hate the water.'

'Now you do know that now you've said that you'll probably end up having to fight off a shark, don't you?'

Mike laughed. 'I don't think we're in Jaws, are we? I don't remember that starting on a train.'

'No, but you've mentioned hating the water, and in movies that sort of statement always leads to the hero having to face his demons in deadly circumstances.'

'I'd like to think my personal demons are well and truly locked up,' said Mike, darkly.

Angela wanted to ask him what he meant by that, but felt she should keep things light. 'Go on, tell me other things about yourself. If you mention enough phobias, the chances are it's unlikely you'll have to face all of them.'

But apart from telling her he had been in the army, he was remarkably shady about what he had done since leaving. 'You're a spy,' guessed Angela.

'I am not a spy.'

'Yes, you are. That's why you won't tell me what you do for a living. You're on the train because . . . ' Angela paused to give herself time to come up with something good. 'Someone is stealing priceless icons from Eastern Europe and you're here to stop them.'

'Except we're on our way to Eastern Europe,' said Mike. 'I hardly think they would be taking the icons back, do you? But I'm very flattered you believe I'd be involved in such an exciting career.'

'Hmm,' said Angela. 'Okay, not a spy. Someone has planted a McGuffin on the train and . . . ' McGuffin was the word Hitchcock had coined for an object or abstract article that drove a story but was not, in itself, relevant. Like the falcon in *The Maltese Falcon*, or the tune that the old lady had memorised in *The Lady Vanishes*, which turned out to be an important clause in a political document.

At the next table, Monsieur Ambroise, who was serving crepe suzette to the diners, dropped the frying pan with a clatter, spreading blue fire all over. It singed his tunic slightly and caused the female diner to squeal. 'Excuse me, madame, monsieur,' he said, flicking at his tunic with a napkin. 'Cal, come 'ere.'

The young blond boy walked down the carriage. 'Finish this, while I clean up.'

'No problemo,' said Cal. He winked at Angela as he passed their table. He certainly fancies himself, though Angela. It amused her, but there was something about his arrogance that she did not like.

'I must go somewhere,' said Ambroise. 'You understand?'

'I understand.'

'So please will you take care of the passengers?'

Angela had forgotten what she was saying, struck by the little scene she had just witnessed. She suspected that something had upset Monsieur Ambroise, but she was perplexed by how he almost seemed to be asking Cal's permission to go. She leaned forward to Mike in a conspiratorial manner.

'Are you sure you're not a spy?' she whispered.

'Definitely not,' said Mike, putting his hands together under his chin, almost as if in prayer. 'That was a bit interesting, wasn't it?' He shook his head. 'No, I'm not going there. I've come away from Stony End to get away from intrigue.'

'Really? What sort of intrigue?'

'Oh you know, the usual. Murder, arson, dropping litter.'

'You too?' Angela opened her eyes wide. 'I thought only Midchester was like that.'

They spent the rest of dinner discussing all the crimes that had happened in their respective home villages, both of which seemed to be hotbeds of lust, greed and general wickedness behind the cottages covered in wisteria. But whereas Midchester was in Shropshire, Stony End was in the Peak District.

'We have Roman ruins,' said Angela. 'A victim was buried in them for twenty years.'

'We have a castle,' said Mike. 'As far as I know no one is buried there, but it was supposed to be a Roundhead stronghold during the Civil War. We did find someone buried under the goal-posts on the recreation ground once.'

'Ooh,' said Angela. 'That's interesting. My mum and dad were involved in uncovering a crime not so long ago,' Angela told Mike. 'It was about a schoolgirl who went missing in the sixties.'

'I think I read about that in the paper,' said Mike. 'Isn't the film going to star Matt Damon and Emily Blunt?'

Angela laughed. 'I don't doubt it! Go on, your turn. What's the most interesting crime that's happened in Stony End?'

'Oh,' he said, his eyes clouding over. 'Nothing as interesting as missing schoolgirls and cat burglars, I'm afraid.'

It was obvious that Mike was keeping something from her. Something different this time. She tried to remember where she had heard the name Stony End recently, but the more she tried to think, the more she came up blank. The alcohol had not helped.

'I've had too much to drink,' she said, pushing away her glass of wine.

'Yes, me too. How about some coffee?'

'I'd love some. But maybe we could go and drink it in the cabin? I mean, you know, because it's more comfortable.' It occurred to Angela he may think she was coming on to him. And what if you are, a little voice inside her head asked. It had been a long time since she had met such a fascinating and charming man. She shook her head, unaware of how her Titian curls moved and glowed in the soft lighting of the dining car. She was not a one night stand sort of woman, and if it turned out to be awful she had nowhere to go to escape. It would be better to keep things formal and business-like.

'What are you thinking?' asked Mike.

'I'm thinking that sometimes I wish I wasn't such a good girl,' she said, before she could stop herself.

'You've also had rather a lot to drink,' said Mike, softly, putting his hand over hers. He made her feel safe and secure in a very silly, girly sort of way that normally would make her laugh at herself.

47

'Meaning?'

'Meaning there are rules about these things and I'm not about to break them.'

'Thank you. That's the most gentlemanly brush off I've ever had.'

'It's not a brush off. You have no idea how difficult it is for me to refuse those wonderful curls and those lovely lips. I'm saying that now is not the right time and I don't want to spoil anything.'

'Thank you, Mike.' For some reason the kindness in his voice made Angela feel like crying. 'Oh dear,' she said, wiping her eyes. 'I really have had too much to drink, haven't I?'

'Come on, Miss Cunningham,' he said, gallantly. 'I'll see you safely to the cabin then I'll come back here and have a coffee at the bar while you get ready for bed.'

* * *

Mike sat at the bar, drinking scotch on the rocks, and trying not to rush back to Angela. She really was delightful. For an actress she did not seem to have any idea just how lovely she was. With her Titian curls, blue-green eyes and sensual lips, she could still stop traffic. She was sexy without even trying to be. More than once he had noticed the other men in the restaurant car giving her second, third and fourth glances.

He began to wish he had been more honest with her. After all, her father was a vicar, so she would understand that they were men just like other men. On the other hand, her father, who would probably be elderly, could be one of those arid high church types, who droned on about religion without actually feeling the strength of the words. Not that Andrew Cunningham had seemed that way when his daughter spoke about him.

Mike had rather enjoyed Angela thinking he could be a spy, and so had kept silent, afraid she would find him boring if she knew the truth. Now he wondered how he could possibly tell her the truth. The obvious time to do so was when she told him about her father. Might she not wonder why he had kept it a secret? Perhaps she would understand if he explained it to her. He had enjoyed being with her and flirting with her, without his dog collar forming a barrier between them. In his experience, which was admittedly limited since Julia died, women suddenly turned back into virgins when they found out his profession. He was the ecclesiastical equivalent of James Bond, turning bad girls good.

Not that Angela was a bad girl in any way. But he had enjoyed the way she looked at him with obvious desire. He took a sip of his whisky and laughed at his own conceit. She had had rather a lot to drink. Maybe in the morning, she would look at him again and wonder what on earth made her flirt with him in the first place. He hoped not. He also desired her, and even if they were both too mature and sensible to have a fling, he would like to think he might see her again when their journey was over.

He looked up and saw the young porter called Cal was at the other end of the bar, chatting up two girls. The head porter, Ambroise had returned wearing a clean tunic, but still looking flustered.

What had gone on there, Mike wondered, then tried to push the feeling aside. He was supposed to be taking a break, and whatever was happening was nothing to do with him whatsoever. Even if there was a McGuffin, as Angela called it, on the train, let them get on with it. They could smuggle whatever they liked as long as he reached Cariastan and had the break from everything as he had promised himself. He wondered how long Angela planned to stay in Cariastan. Perhaps they could go sightseeing together. First he would have to be honest with her about his profession. He could not start any romance on a false footing.

His natural curiosity allowed him about five minutes of pretending not to care about what was happening on the train, and having Angela filling his thoughts made it easier to push it all aside. But eventually he started to wonder again what was going on, if anything. He was certain that when Ambroise dropped the crepe pan, it was because of what Angela had said about there being a McGuffin on the train. But why? It was obviously a joke. If she had said there was a cache of jewels or weapons on the train and had come close to the truth, then Ambroise's behaviour made sense. Or if he had dropped the pan when she mentioned the icons. But it had happened after she mentioned there being a 'something' on the train. It suggested that the head porter was very frightened about that something indeed.

Ambroise rubbed his forehead with a handkerchief as he passed Mike at the bar. Not only was he terrified, he was sweating profusely.

When Ambroise received a text message a few moments later, as he was serving at a table, Mike made a decision to follow as Ambroise dashed from the dining car, calling to Cal to take charge again.

Mike bought a packet of cigarettes and a lighter from Cal, grimacing as he said, 'I was supposed to be giving up'. Then he smiled and murmured a friendly goodnight to people as he passed their tables, trying to act as if he were just leaving to go to his cabin. Nothing would appear more natural, especially as Ambroise was going in that direction. He hoped they would all think he was rushing off to be with Angela, though he felt a pang of guilt in case it gave her a bad name.

He followed the head porter through several of the carriages in which the cabins were situated, and saw him go into one at the far end, where the truly luxury cabins were. Mike passed the young woman with the child, who was still in the passageway, presumably to give the little boy more room to run around than the tiny cabin she had booked. She smiled tightly as Mike went past, and then pulled the child to her. Mike was not offended. He understood it was what every mother did to protect her offspring when a strange man was in the vicinity of her child. Or, he thought grimly, it was what every mother should do. It did occur to him that a child of that age should be tucked up in bed, but maybe the movement of the train was making it difficult for the little one to sleep.

He shook that thought away, more interested in what Ambroise was up to. If indeed he was up to anything. Mike remembered that he had missed the obvious signs before, because he was too busy being sympathetic and supportive. He would not allow that to happen again. He stopped near to the luxury cabin and opened the window in the corridor slightly, letting in some night air. He took out the cigarettes and lighter, in case the young mum was watching him and made a great play of not being sure whether to light it up or not. Inside the train was completely non-smoking, but he had seen a couple of people with their heads half out the window, unable to give up their daily dose of nicotine.

Mike had not smoked since he was in the army. He had given up because his role at the time made smoking rather a dangerous occupation. He hoped that he would not really have to take a puff of the cigarette in order to prove to the girl that he was indeed just stopping for a smoke.

Instead, he leaned against the wall, and could just about make out voices coming from the cabin. Unfortunately, he soon realised, they were all speaking in Russian and he did not have a clue what was being said. He could not help longing for a spy film scenario where the bad guys — if indeed they were bad guys — helpfully detailed all their dastardly plans in broken English, despite the fact there was no reason they should not speak in their mother tongue.

The walls to the cabins were so thin that if they had been speaking in English, he would have heard everything.

Even though Mike could not understand Russian, he understood the inflections that people used when they were winding up a conversation. So he hastily pulled the window down further, and lit up a cigarette, turning his back to the girl with the child, so she could not see that he was not actually dragging on it.

Ambroise left the cabin, still flustered and sweating. He stood looking at Mike disapprovingly. 'There is no smoking allowed on the train, Monsieur.' He pointed to the no-smoking sign.

'Yeah, sorry,' said Mike, throwing the untouched cigarette out of the window. 'I'm supposed to be giving up anyway.'

Ambroise nodded politely, and went back down the corridor towards the restaurant car. As he passed the young mum, the child put his arms up to Ambroise, almost as if he knew him. The mother pulled him back even more briskly than she had when Mike passed her. He could not see Ambroise's face, as the porter had his back to him, but he could have sworn that the man's shoulders slumped.

Mike was about to move when he saw the young mum heading in his direction, carrying the child, who was crying softly. To his amazement, they went into the cabin that Ambroise had just exited.

He was moving away when he heard the girl say, in English, 'A man was in the corridor. I think he was listening to you.'

'What man?' a voice snapped in a strong Russian accent.

'The tall English man. The one the woman in the restaurant said looks like a spy.' Mike heard movement in the cabin.

He legged it then, moving through the carriages as fast as he could back to the cabin he shared with Angela. A burst of adrenalin he had not experienced for many years helped to quicken his steps. In the army they had called it the fight or flight gene. Back then he might have stayed to fight, but without knowing the lay of the land on the train, he had no choice but to run away, at least until he found out what was going on. He managed to shut the door before he heard the door at the end of their carriage open.

It would give him little respite from the danger he sensed in every nerve. The girl knew what he looked like. Ambroise would undoubtedly know his name, or find it out very quickly from the passenger manifest.

With the train not stopping again until the morning, Mike had nowhere else to go.

3

Angela had dozed off, and awoke startled when Mike shook her awake. Her first thought was whether or not she had been drooling in her sleep. Her hand went to her mouth to check.

'I'm sorry,' he whispered. 'I need to speak to you.'

'Why? What's wrong?' Angela sat up, awkwardly crouching under the bunk bed. Mike folded the top bunk back, giving them both more room to sit. He put his finger to his lips, because Angela had spoken in a loud voice.

'You're right,' he murmured. 'Something is going on here. I don't know what, but I'm worried. I think the child is involved somehow.'

She listened as he quickly filled her in on what had happened since she went to bed. 'Do you really think the child knows Ambroise?' she asked.

'I'm certain of it. He wanted Ambroise to lift him up and give him a cuddle. I couldn't see Ambroise's face, but I think he was devastated when the woman snatched the kiddie back. And there are the mysterious Russians in the most expensive carriage.'

'Mike,' said Angela, in a placatory tone, 'it's really late, and I was being silly talking about McGuffins. I suppose I wanted to think we were in some sort of adventure together. But I'm sure there's nothing wrong really. The Russians are probably really rich and demanding, hence Ambroise having to run whenever they call. No wonder the poor man looks flustered. The child is friendly with everyone. I honestly think he'd have come with me this afternoon if I'd asked him.'

'And what about the girl, telling them I was listening?'

'Well . . . you were, weren't you? I suppose we'd want to know if anyone was listening to us.'

'Hmm,' said Mike, pursing his lips.

'You're probably right. We reach Innsbruck in the morning. When we get there, I'll get off the train and have a word with someone at the station. Just to set my own mind at rest.'

'That's a good idea, if you're really worried.'

Mike laughed softly, and stood up to pull his bed out. 'You're absolutely right, of course. I'm putting two and two together and coming up with the plot of a Hitchcock film.'

'That's what you get for hanging around with actresses.'

'Yes, I shall have to choose my travelling companions more carefully in future.'

'Oh,' said Angela, feeling a little hurt. She lay back on her pillow, deflated.

Mike carried on straightening up his bed, talking at the same time. 'If I will insist on sharing a cabin with a beautiful, fascinating woman, you can hardly blame me for thinking I'm in some sort of fantasy.'

He climbed up onto the bed, but

Angela noticed he did not undress. She was grateful for that. She was not sure she could cope with seeing his broad shoulders in the flesh, as it were. She might make a complete fool of herself by trying to seduce him. His tone of voice, though very flattering, said that he thought the whole thing was a joke. She did not want to be the punch-line.

Angela lay awake well into the night, thinking about what Mike had told her. From an early age, her mother and father had taught her to notice things. She had not seen as much as Mike, but she had indeed noticed Ambroise's reaction when she mentioned a McGuffin on the train. She did not really notice him until then, but she felt pretty certain that he knew how to cook a crepe, and she was just as certain he was practised enough never to drop the pan. So something had spooked him. He looked like a man who had been given a death sentence.

She also took to thinking about the girl with the child. The woman was protective, yes. Probably exhausted too. But loving? Angela had no experience of motherhood, but she had friends who did. Sometimes their offspring exasperated them, but the love was always there, in the background. She did not sense that with the girl and little Solomon.

Then she began to think of Solomon and Ambroise, Ambroise and Solomon. Their names coursed through her head, along with their faces.

'It's his grandson,' she said aloud. 'They have the same cleft chin.'

'That's just what I was thinking,' said Mike, proving he too had been lying awake ruminating on what happened. 'Or they're related in some way.'

'The girl is working for the Russians,' said Angela. 'And they're holding the child as collateral. But for what? If they were smuggling jewels or drugs, they could do that better without Ambroise knowing. It's got to be something big. Something they need his help with.'

'The drivers are usually changed in

each country,' said Mike. 'It says so on the brochure.'

'So how could Ambroise stop that happening?'

'My guess is that he knows all the drivers, and would probably know if someone was there who shouldn't be.'

'That can't be it,' said Angela. 'They must have new drivers sometimes.'

'I should think so for a trip lasting thirty hours.'

'Unless there are just two, and one sleeps whilst the other drives. Eight hours on or eight hours off.' Angela got out of bed, forgetting she was only wearing her nightie. It did not matter. She threw her jeans on and tucked the nightie into them, then put on a thick sweater. 'I'm having real trouble sleeping,' she said. 'I may go for a walk to clear my head.'

Mike jumped down off his bed. 'You're not going alone.'

'My hero. I was hoping you'd say that.'

'Angela, look. I need to tell you the

truth about myself . . . '

'No you don't. We don't have time for confessions anyway. We need to find out what is going on here, if anything. Come on. While everyone is sleeping.'

Angela opened the door to the corridor and looked out. She nodded to Mike to let him know the coast was clear.

'Where shall we start?' she murmured as they closed and locked the cabin door.

'Let's start at the very beginning,' he said, pointing towards the front end of the train. 'We'll have to walk through the buffet car, but I doubt anyone will be around at this time of night.'

Angela nodded her agreement and followed him along the carriage. She could not help wondering about the little boy, and whether he really was in danger. On the other hand, Angela realised she had jumped to a very swift conclusion, based on nothing more than what Mike had told her about the child wanting to be picked up by

Ambroise, and the fact that both had cleft chins. It was hardly the stuff of which crime convictions were made.

'It doesn't make sense,' she said to Mike as they walked through the carriage. 'The woman and the child are English but Ambroise is French. So maybe we're completely wrong.'

'Yes, there is that,' Mike agreed. 'But there's no reason why his daughter couldn't be English, if he married an English woman. Or his son is French, but the girl is a daughter-in-law.'

'That could be it. Maybe they've just had a fall out, and she's keeping the child from him. Or maybe we should stop playing spies and go back to bed.' Angela became flustered. 'I mean, we should each go back to our own bunk.' It all seemed a bit silly now she was up and about, especially as the train was so quiet, with everyone else fast asleep.

'We're up now,' said Mike. 'We might as well get a drink in the buffet car.'

'I've had too much to drink. That's probably why I'm following you through a train in the middle of the night, in search of a McGuffin, and making up connections between a man and a child based on specious reasoning.'

'Coffee then?'

'Yes, coffee would be nice. Or a nice cup of tea.'

'I can't promise a *nice* cup of tea. We are in Europe after all. I'm pretty certain they use all the tea-leaves that Tetley threw out.'

'Yes,' Angela said, grimacing. 'You do have a point.'

When they reached the buffet car, Mike stood back and let Angela go ahead of him. Always the gentleman.

There was a tired and rather ragged looking couple sitting in one of the booths. They were well-dressed. Probably over-dressed compared to many of the passengers, who wore casual clothes, but their eyes were tired and the woman looked very pale. She was blonde, with one of those concrete hairstyles favoured by American First Ladies. The man was balding, with spectacles.

They looked up when they saw Angela. They smiled politely at her in the way English people do when they are abroad. She doubted they would exchange more than a few words with her on the journey. Then she noticed they looked beyond her and their smiles became more familiar and welcoming.

'Reverend Fairfax, there you are!' exclaimed the woman.

Angela turned her head, only half-registering the surname she had only heard once that day. She was therefore expecting to see that someone else had entered the buffet car. But the only person behind her was Mike.

She raised her eyebrows. 'Reverend?'

4

Mike very quickly made introductions, trying to ignore Angela's questioning glance. 'Liberty and Harry Cathcart, this is Angela Cunningham. Liberty and Harry live in my village.'

'It's very nice to meet you,' said Angela, through tight lips. Mike hoped he would get a chance to explain soon. He did not want her to think he had misled her for dubious reasons.

'Why don't you both join us?' Liberty Cathcart said icily. She was looking at Angela as if she were some sort of alien creature. Mike had seen that look before, whenever any woman in the village took an interest in him. He did not believe that Liberty fancied him, but she seemed determined to vet all his relationships for him. 'You didn't tell us you had a new ... friend, Michael,' she added, with a note of reproach in her voice. Her use of his first name was clearly meant to show that she was on intimate terms with him.

'We've only just met,' Angela said. 'We're hardly friends at all.'

Oh dear, thought Mike.

'I didn't realise you'd be on this train,' he said, struggling to retain his good humour. 'You didn't mention it when I called in to ask you to look after the cat.'

'It was a last minute idea,' said Liberty, unabashed. 'I said to Harry that we can't have you going off all on your own. Especially after . . . well, you know. We would have found you sooner, but I was terribly ill after the flight to Nice, and all I wanted to do was sit in the cabin with a cold compress over my eyes. Would you believe that young porter wanted us to swap because some man and woman didn't want to share? I presume they were some lovers who had a fall out. I told him, 'We've paid for two bunks in the same cabin and we're sticking to them.' As if they would separate a devoted husband and wife.'

'Actually that was us,' said Angela with another tight smile. 'We found out we were sharing by accident, so it was definitely not a tiff between lovers. We've just had to make do and put up with each other.'

'Oh.' Liberty's eyes opened wide in shock. 'Well, of course we shall swap. Harry will go in with Mike and I'll share with Audrey.'

'Angela,' Mike and Angela said together.

'That's nice, dear.'

'Actually,' said Angela, her eyes flashing with anger, 'we're fine. We're both grown-ups after all, and we've managed so far.'

'Even so,' said Liberty. 'With Michael being a vicar . . . well, if word got back to Stony End . . . No, it's decided. We'll swap. Go and get your things, Amelia.'

'I don't want to, Lillian,' said Angela, clearly fuming. Mike cringed with embarrassment, but more for Angela's

71

sake than Liberty Cathcart's. He knew that Liberty could be strident, and a little bit bossy, but he had never known her to behave so rudely towards anyone.

'It's Liberty.'

'That's nice, dear,' said Angela in sweet, but deadly, tones. Her point was lost on Liberty, who never saw anything wrong in her own behaviour, but was always quick to judge others.

'Coffee, Angela?' said Mike, remembering why they had gone to the buffet car. He doubted they would have a chance to search the train now the Cathcarts had decided to follow him.

'Not for me,' said Angela, standing up. Mike had to move out of his seat to let her pass. 'I'm going back to get some sleep.'

'I thought we were changing carriages,' said Harry Cathcart, who seemed to have had trouble keeping up. That was normal for Harry. He let Liberty ride roughshod over him, and seldom had much to say in defence.

'We're not,' said Angela, leaving all three of them sitting there.

Mike spent half an hour chatting to the Cathcarts, listening to all their woes about having to travel economy on the plane to Nice.

'Really, I'm not a snob,' said Liberty. 'But the way some people go on nowadays. No one dresses to travel anymore.' Mike looked down at his own jeans and sweater. 'Oh, not you, Michael. Of course you always look like the right sort.'

'The right sort?'

'Well, refined and well-bred, of course.'

'Actually my mother was an alcoholic and my father left her when she was three months pregnant,' he said. 'We lived on a council estate in Bromley and half the time she couldn't pay the rent because she spent it on booze. I left at sixteen to go into army training college and never looked back. I don't know if she's dead or alive.' It was a shame he lived with, knowing that as a man of the church he should forgive, but finding it impossible in his mother's case.

'Oh, well, you've done well for yourself then,' said Liberty. 'You became the right sort and that's what matters.'

Tired of talk about the 'right sort', Mike excused himself and went back to the cabin. He ignored Liberty's protestations about him sharing with Angela and it not being correct for a man of his standing.

This time he did not disturb Angela, though he suspected that she was awake. He could almost hear her quietly fuming.

He climbed up on to his bunk and lay down, fully clothed.

'Goodnight, Reverend,' she said. He would have answered, but he heard her turning over and thumping her pillow. He was afraid then that he might be the next thing she thumped.

★ ★ ★

'We need to talk,' Mike said the next morning, when they had both washed and changed their clothes.

'No we don't, Reverend,' said Angela, looking in the mirror and brushing her luscious curls until they shone. 'Or should I call you Matthew?' She was clearly still very angry about Liberty's rudeness in deliberately getting her name wrong and what she saw as his lies.

'See,' said Mike, irritated. 'That's exactly what we need to talk about. Because now you know that, you obviously feel it's the only thing about me that you do know. But I'm more than just the job I do, Angela.'

'You lied to me.'

'No, I didn't. I just omitted to tell you I was a vicar.'

'It's the same thing. It's not as if vicars weren't mentioned, Mike. I told you my father is one. Well, he's retired, but he's still a vicar at heart. That was your cue to say 'I'm a vicar too.' Somehow you forgot to mention it.' It did not

75

surprise him that she had exactly the same thought process as him.

'And what does that mean, Angela? Putting aside your dad for a minute, what exactly does me being a vicar mean? Does it mean I can't be attracted to you? That I can't wish I could run my fingers through those curls? Or kiss those wonderful lips? Does it mean that I can't possibly want to make love to you?'

She turned to face him, wide-eyed, as a blush stole across her cheeks. 'No, of course not. Only it wouldn't be right. Would it?' She frowned, but even that made her look lovely.

He moved closer to her and put his hand on her waist, pulling her to him. 'At this moment in time, it feels like the only right thing to do.'

'Lucretia would be very upset if we did.' Despite her joke at Liberty's expense, Angela's voice trembled.

'Oh well, it's worth it just for that.' He bent down and lightly touched her lips with his.

She put her hand on his chest, and pushed him away playfully. 'I'm not letting you make love to me just to upset Lola.'

'Then what about because you want me as much as I want you? Or is that just wishful thinking on my part?'

'Yes, that works for me.' She put her arms around his neck and pulled him back to her. This time the kiss they shared was more passionate, full of the desire they had both been holding back.

'Am I forgiven?' Mike murmured against her mouth.

'I haven't decided yet.' Angela kissed him again.

Any hopes they might have had of becoming intimate were rudely interrupted by a hammering on the cabin door. 'Come to the restaurant car now. Everyone. Come. Come.' They heard Ambroise knocking on more doors.

'What the hell . . . ?' said Mike.

Everyone trooped into the restaurant car. As the train was full, so was the carriage. Some people had to stand at the back, because there were not quite enough restaurant tables. It was seldom expected that everyone would dine at the same time.

Mike noticed that there were train staff amongst those assembled in the restaurant car. Everyone chatted, looking nervous. Harry and Liberty Cathcart were also there, looking even more exhausted than before. They smiled wanly at Mike, but whilst Harry nodded politely at Angela, Liberty practically ignored her.

'I wonder if it's like that film,' said Will, moving over to Mike and Angela. 'You know, *The Cassandra Crossing*. The one with the deadly virus on that train.'

'I haven't seen anyone being ill,' said Angela. It said something about both Mike and Angela's state of mind that they did not scoff at Will's idea. At the moment it was anybody's guess as to what was going on.

Ambroise entered the restaurant car, closely followed by the girl and the little boy. After them came a big man, flanked by several bigger men, all of whom were carrying machine guns. No one had to be told the man front and centre was in charge. He had a dominant bearing. His fierce looks were made fiercer by the fact that he had a scar all the way down his left cheek.

'Silence!' he said, even though it was not necessary. Everyone had stopped talking to look at him. Mike recognised his voice as being the one he heard coming from the luxury cabin the night before. 'My name is Dmitri Karloff.'

'Not his real name,' Will whispered.

Karloff glared at him, and Will visibly shrank. Angela put her hand on the boy's shoulder, to comfort him. 'My name is Dmitri Karloff,' he repeated. 'I am a citizen of Cariastan. This train has been taken over. Hijacked. As such it will not stop in Innsbruck or at any other station on the way to Cariastan. We will press on, and when we arrive in Cariastan at midnight tonight . . . '

It was on Mike's mind to point out

that if they did not make their designated stops, either they would run out of fuel or they would reach Cariastan earlier.

It was almost as if Karloff read his mind. 'I promise we will arrive at midnight.'

'You want to stop the coronation,' said Angela.

'You are very wise, madam,' said Karloff. 'I will not allow my country to step back in time. We will become no more than serfs and subjects.'

'Actually,' said Harry Cathcart, 'Prince Henri is very forward thinking. He believes in the will of the people, as his father did, but he also understands that Cariastan appears to work better with a monarchy. It will bring tourism and more jobs to the country.'

'Harry,' said Liberty, reproachfully. 'What on earth do you know of politics?'

'I'm a parish councillor,' said Harry, defensively. 'And I read the newspaper.'

'Yes, well we're not talking about the

church fund now. So do be quiet before that awful man shoots us.'

Harry visibly shrank in front of his more forceful wife.

'We do not plan to shoot anyone, Mrs . . . ' Karloff paused as one of the men whispered in his ear. 'Cathcart. Oh yes. A very interesting lady indeed. Perhaps madam, you should be quiet.'

Mike frowned. There was something about Karloff's tone of voice that he did not like. He liked even less that Liberty seemed to curl up and wither at the terrorist's remark. Mike was used to her being very forthright indeed.

'So,' said Angela, 'now you've proved you know everything about us all. I mean, I'm assuming you do.'

'I do indeed, Miss Cunningham, and whilst I did not watch *Pandora's Vox* when it was on the television, I intend to watch it as soon as this is all over.'

'So obviously you're planning on getting out of this alive,' said Angela. 'So where does that leave us? Are we to be hostages until Prince Anton agrees to cancel the coronation?'

Karloff nodded gallantly. 'As I said, Miss Cunningham, you are very wise.'

'Are you planning to let the women and children go?' asked Mike. 'If you want sympathy for your cause it would be the kindest thing to do.'

'Yes,' said Karloff, rubbing his chin. 'That would be a kind thing to do.' Mike wondered why he did not curl his moustache whilst he was at it. Karloff's performance as an evil overlord was very measured indeed. Angela glanced at Mike and he could see that she was trying to get a message across with her eyes.

'You're not really in charge here, are you?' asked Mike.

'I assure you I am in charge.'

'No,' said Angela. 'You're too bad an actor for that. I doubt real villains stroke their chins or behave with such practised gallantry to women. So what are you? An actor? It's not April the first, is it? Or are we on *Candid Camera*?'

'I am not an actor,' said Karloff, savagely. But Mike knew then that Angela had hit the nail on the head. 'Very well, I may be an actor, but that does not mean I do not have a social conscience. You have your own Vanessa Redgrave, do you not? She is a very admirable woman.'

'Yes, she's wonderful, but I don't think she's ever hijacked a train,' said Angela. 'And nor would she.'

'I'm going to ask you again,' said Mike. 'You must know by now that I'm a vicar. A man of God. It is my duty, therefore, to ensure that everyone on this train remains safe.'

'That is not all you are, is it, Reverend Fairfax?' Karloff grinned.

'Oh for goodness sake,' Angela snapped. 'So you've got Google. Do stop showing off about it and say what you really think. What is he? A vicar kissogram or something? A CIA agent, masquerading as a vicar? A . . . '

'Angela,' said Mike. The dreadful truth was beginning to dawn on him. It

83

was the real reason that Ambroise and Karloff had been talking about him in the carriage.

'What?'

'Do shut up, darling.'

'What? You're not CIA are you? Are you? Or MI5? Or a boy scout? Come on, Mike, you're being as enigmatic as Boris Karloff there.'

'It is Dmitri,' said Karloff.

'Whatever,' said Angela.

'Handcuff him,' Karloff said to one of his men. 'You' He pointed to Harry and Liberty, who were sitting in a booth. 'Move from there now. Handcuff Fairfax and attach the other side to the inside table leg.'

The legs were fixed to the floor, which meant that once Mike was handcuffed and in place, he would not be able to move. That meant he could not stop the awful thing that was going to happen.

'I won't be handcuffed,' he argued, even whilst knowing that it was pointless to do so. 'Just let me stay free and I promise I won't cause any problems.'

'Really, Fairfax and you a man of God? How could you tell such a blatant lie?'

'Okay, I may scream in a minute,' said Angela. 'After all, that's just what this scene is missing. A screaming woman.'

'You're not helping,' said Liberty. 'Why don't you sit down, Andrea and let the men sort this out?'

'Would you prefer me to faint, Lynette?' said Angela, waspishly.

'I'm sorry, Angela, but you're not helping,' Mike whispered. He immediately knew he was wrong to have sided with Liberty. As if they did not have enough to worry about, he had to try and referee two women who had taken an instant dislike to each other.

'Well, maybe that's because I'm terrified, Mike, like everyone else in this carriage. We are all in this situation together. Meanwhile you and Boris here are doing the ultimate alpha male thing of knowing everything whilst failing to share anything. So if someone doesn't tell me what's happening soon, I think I've earned the right to scream.'

There was a murmur of approval from the other passengers and crew. Even Liberty looked as if she thought Angela had a point.

Mike pulled Angela aside. 'I am trying to prevent a panic here,' he whispered.

'You don't think we're past the panicking stage with the whole being hijacked thing?'

'Things can and will get worse,' he said in a low voice.

'How worse?'

'I told you I was in the army, right?'

'Yes.'

'Only I didn't tell you which regiment.'

'No, you didn't. What were you, SAS? Is that it?'

Mike shook his head. He moved in closer and pressed his lips against her ear. 'Bomb squad.'

He watched as his words hit home and dark realisation showed on Angela's face. 'Oh God . . . ' She put her hands to her mouth, and he saw her shudder involuntarily.

'I'm afraid he's not going to help us,' said Mike, grimly. He would not care for himself. He had been in dangerous situations before. His protective instincts took over. He did not want anything to happen to the other passengers. He did not want anything to happen to Angela. He had only just found her, and his mind railed against a God who would play such a trick on him.

'What did he say?' said Liberty Cathcart. 'Michael, you really must tell us all.'

Karloff grinned. 'Reverend Fairfax has just informed Miss Cunningham that he used to be in the bomb squad.' He paused, just as Mike had, for the words to travel around the carriage and hover as apocalyptic clouds above everyone's heads. Some caught on more quickly than others, but the atmosphere in the carriage became electric.

'On this train,' said Karloff, with some ceremony, as if it was the moment he had truly been waiting for, 'is a nuclear device that will explode when the train arrives in Cariastan at midnight.'

5

The future king of Cariastan sat in his study, reading over the government documents which were piled high on his desk. He sighed. There hardly seemed to be enough hours in the day to do what was needed to be done. He wondered if it had been the same for his great-grandfather. He somehow had the idea that in the past kings lived leisurely lives of hunting and fishing, whilst lackeys took care of the day to day running of the country. But he also knew that King Henri the First had been very much a hands-on king. He felt he should honour his great-grandfather by doing the same

He had only met King Henri once, when he was a very small boy. Great-grandfather had been living in exile in Paris. Anton's memory was of a handsome but very elderly man, with a ready smile for his great-grandchild.

His great-grandmother had died and it was just after her funeral that Anton was taken to see the old king. King Henri II did not wait long to join the wife he had adored, passing on only a few weeks later.

The study door opened and a handsome, but rather savage looking man in his thirties entered. He appeared very grave and serious, which was unusual for Faust di Luca. The son of a very old Italian family, Faust was Anton's most trusted advisor. 'Anton, we have a problem,' said Faust.

Whilst the new king would be King Henri III to his people, it was custom in his family for the princes in line to the throne to have a family name. Hence him being known as Prince Anton to all. His great-grandfather had been called Blake.

Faust was one of Anton's oldest friends. They had attended Cambridge together and at one time had fallen in love with twin sisters. Anton wondered where those girls were now. They seemed to belong to a much easier time.

'What is it, Faust?'

Faust paced the floor and ran his fingers through his dark hair, almost as if he was afraid to tell Anton the truth. 'Someone has hijacked the Midnight Train.'

'Dear God.' Anton stood up. 'Who?'

'We don't know, but we've received a demand. They say that if you don't cancel the coronation, then they will detonate a nuclear device when they arrive in Cariastan at midnight tomorrow.'

Anton fell back down into his seat. 'But our security people did checks, didn't they? There are no real threats to my throne? Oh a few old guard from the Soviet era, but I seem to remember that if you offered them a case of the best champagne and Cuban cigars, they soon lost their socialist principles.'

'We don't know who this group is and they don't have a name. But . . . '

Faust hesitated, as if unsure how to break worse news. 'They do have something else. Something very important.'

'What? For God's sake, Faust, just tell me the bad news. As if them threatening the lives of innocent people isn't bad enough.'

'They have your nephew. They say that if you do not call off the coronation, he will die with everyone else.'

Anton shook his head, incredulously. His elder brother, Philipe, had died in a ski-ing accident. If Philipe had lived, he would be the one about to be crowned king. It was only after his brother's death they found out about the child. Anton had been searching for the little boy for over a year. The child was born out of wedlock, so had no real claim on the throne, but that was of no concern to Anton. Family mattered, regardless of legitimacy. That was something his great-grandfather had instilled in everyone in the royal house. Anton had wanted to help the boy, to give him a good home and life in Cariastan, if the child's mother agreed. But attempts to find him had come to nothing. Until now.

'It seems that if I don't call off the coronation, people in Cariastan will die anyway,' said Anton. 'Whatever happens,' he said, going into official mode, 'we need to find out as much as we can about this bomb. How much damage it might do if it does explode? What other countries around us might be affected by the fallout? What are the international implications of it even being in existence? Because if other European states hear of it travelling through their country to get here, then we are going to have to deal with some pretty tough questions.' He shook his head. 'Damn it, we don't even have nuclear capability or weapons of mass destruction, and nor will we as long as I have a say in the matter. But I can't imagine the Americans believing that, can you?'

Faust shrugged miserably. Who knew

what the Americans might do? They might use it as an excuse to invade Cariastan and get another foothold in the region. Anton knew that this was on Faust's mind just as it was on his. He did not want to live under American occupation. Especially as they had recently found oil in the south of the country. Anton wanted the revenue from that to benefit his people, not some big cartel in Texas. 'I'll get everything in motion,' Faust said. 'Don't worry, Anton, we will beat this.'

'Yes, we will. We'll start by cancelling the coronation.'

'I can't believe you're going to give in to the demands of terrorists, Anton. Can't you see what this might do to your plans to rule? Even if we avert a crisis, people might say you are too weak to rule Cariastan.'

'What other option do I have, Faust? There are innocent people on that train, including my nephew, and in every one of the countries it is travelling through. Not to mention what it might do to Cariastan when it arrives. We're only a tiny country after all. It won't take long to wipe us off the map and turn us into a nuclear wasteland.' Anton shuddered at the thought. He wished his great-grandfather were there to share his wisdom. He looked at the picture of the old king over the fireplace, hoping for some kind of sign. His great-grandfather merely looked on benignly. Well, thought Anton, he's probably telling me that I'm on my own. 'No, our first duty is to the innocent people who might be affected by this bomb. The coronation can wait until we have these bastards in custody. Inform the leaders of all the countries that the train travels through of the situation. They need to be ready in case this bomb somehow detonates. What if the train crashes?'

'I'll get all the advice I can,' said Faust. 'The Secretary of Defence is putting together all the information we need and talking to the best people. We'll get through this Anton.'

'I hope so.' Anton went to the telephone. 'I'd better call my mother and tell her about her grandson. While I'm at it, I'll tell her to leave the country. In fact, we need to get everyone out before the train arrives. Find out the best routes for everyone, Faust, and get the military to help them.'

'It's already in hand,' said Faust.

Anton nodded. He should have known Faust would have done everything he could before breaking the bad news. 'Thank you, my friend.'

★ ★ ★

Karloff's announcement about the bomb had been met with the sobbing of women and the tight lips of white-faced men. Angela had to sit down, she felt so weak. Yet she was determined not to be the helpless woman. She could see Mike's face and that he was taking it all upon himself, as if he were personally responsible for everyone on the train.

She needed to be strong for his sake, so that he would have one less person to worry about.

'Cal,' said Karloff, beckoning the young porter. 'Collect all the mobile phones, and laptops, then do a search of the cabins and ensure there are no more.' Everyone had been so shocked by the revelations that no one had thought to use their phones.

'What?' said Will, looking askance at his friend. 'You're in on this?'

'Oh shut up, boy scout,' said Cal. 'If this were a film, you'd be on the losing team. So suck it up.'

'I can't believe it,' said Will. 'I thought you were my friend. We were going to go to uni together.'

'This pays better,' said Cal, as he collected up the phones and gadgets as per Karloff's instructions.

'You don't need the money,' said Will. 'Your father is rich. You've got more money than you know what to do with.'

'There's no such thing as having too

much money,' said Cal.

'When the search is complete, you may return to your cabins,' said Karloff, cutting into the discussion. 'There you will stay until such time as we need to see you. You will be fed, but only cold food and you will receive drinks. And the good news,' he said, spreading his arms, 'is that it is all for free!'

'Whoopee do,' said the ageing rocker with the blond lion's mane hair.

They handcuffed Mike to one of the tables. Angela insisted they brought him a drink and food. When the search of the cabins had ended, culminating in a pile of phones, laptops and other Wi-Fi enabled equipment at the end of the restaurant car, Angela refused to go back to hers.

'I'm staying with Mike,' she said, sitting down opposite him.

'You will do as you are told,' said Karloff.

'I will not. I'm staying with him. Or you can bring him to the cabin and handcuff him there. After all, where are we going to go? The windows are sealed.'

'Yes, but women have pins for their hair, or on their brooches,' said Karloff. 'I too watch television, Miss Cunningham.'

'But you clearly know nothing about fashion,' said Angela, derisively. 'Women don't wear those pins anymore. They certainly don't wear brooches, unless they're eighty years old. And I assure you that whilst I may be getting on a bit, I am not that old.' She shook her curls out to illustrate. 'See? Not a pin in sight.'

'If it means I do not have to put up with you talking at me, then take him!' Karloff turned to one of his lackeys. 'Take him!'

A few minutes later, Mike was handcuffed, rather uncomfortably to the top bunk. As he was sitting on the bottom bunk, it meant his arm was raised above his head. Karloff's lackeys went out and locked the door from the outside. Angela listened to make sure they walked away. She heard them talking in the distance, then the door to the restaurant car opening and closing.

'Angela,' said Mike. 'Do me a favour.'

'What? Do you need a pillow? Or a blanket?'

'No, I need you to stop trying to help me. Whilst I was in the restaurant car, I could hear what was going on. Now I can't. It was also marginally more comfortable being handcuffed to the leg of the table than now with my hand stuck above my head.'

'Oh you're just as much of an idiot as Karloff is,' she said, with mock disdain. She pulled out her overnight bag and went into her make up case. It had been searched, but not very thoroughly, but that was only because the men had not known what to look for. She took out her compact, and proceeded to open it and snap the top from the bottom, breaking the mechanism. A bright, gold-coloured pin, roughly two inches long, fell out of the joint on the compact and onto the bed. 'When I was in *Pandora's Vox*,' she said, as she picked up the pin and reached up to the handcuffs, 'I had to learn to do certain tricks. We didn't have computer graphics in those days. So a magician taught me all sorts of stuff. One of which was how to undo handcuffs. I used that trick in *Pandora Meets Houdini*.' She fiddled with the handcuffs. 'And now,' she said, as the lock on the handcuffs finally clicked back, 'I've used it here.'

Mike rubbed his hand and then stroked Angela's face. 'I'm sorry.'

'Hmm,' she murmured, getting up off the bed quickly. 'You're expecting me to forgive rather a lot. First that you lied to me about your profession and since then you've twice, in the last half an hour or so, tried to put me into my place as the little woman who should not speak until she is spoken to.'

'That wasn't my intention. My intention was to stop them shooting you.'

'Well as you can see,' she said, holding up the pin. 'I'm quite capable of taking care of myself.'

'I don't think that pin would help much against a couple of machine guns, darling.'

'Stop it. You haven't earned the right to call me darling yet. Besides it's distracting. We need to work out now how to get out of here and what we're going to do when we do. You'll defuse the bomb of course. I mean, if you can. Are nuclear bombs the same as ordinary bombs?'

'It depends whether it's a nuclear bomb or just a dirty bomb. It's more likely to be the latter, as it's easier to set off. A proper nuclear bomb would probably need some sort of rocket launcher.'

'What is a dirty bomb?'

'It's an ordinary bomb, but has radioactive material in it. So as well as the initial explosion, which could be massive, it floods the air with radiation.'

'Oh God . . . ' Angela sat on the edge of the bunk. 'I don't really like either idea. But you have until we reach

Cariastan to find out and defuse it.'

'I doubt that very much, Angela. If the future king is the man I think he is, it's his duty to inform those countries we pass through.' Mike picked up the Midnight Train tourist brochure that was in a little stand on the tiny table in the cabin. 'We're in Austria at the moment.' He traced the route. 'We'll pass through these countries, here, here and here, before we reach Cariastan. None of the countries are going to want a live nuclear device passing through their land with the chance that it could be detonated at any time.'

'Which means?' Angela slumped down on the seat at the side of the table.

'They may take the decision to blow up the train.'

'But won't that detonate the bomb anyway?'

'It depends what sort of bomb it is. If it's a nuclear warhead, then no, it won't go off just because they blow up the train. It needs a particular reaction. You could jump up and down on the end of a nuclear warhead, and nothing will happen. If it's a dirty bomb, that's a bit different. It has radioactive material attached to it, which could be released into the atmosphere.'

'So are we hoping it's a nuclear warhead?' Angela raised an eyebrow, horrified by their situation.

'In a way, yes. Whatever happens, they will probably pick an area where not many people live. There are plenty of places like that where we're travelling. Miles and miles of fields and mountain regions. And then they can send a hazmat team in to lessen the effects of the radiation if it is a dirty bomb. They'll also want to try and get the terrorists too, and my guess is that Karloff and his people will bail out long before Cariastan. They don't look the suicidal type to me.'

'They have to get off the train . . . ' Angela mused. 'So they'll have arranged a pick up point, won't they?'

'Exactly,' said Mike. 'But the people

on the outside don't know where that pick up point will be, or even whether the terrorists are willing to die for their cause. If one of the countries we pass through blows up the train first, they can . . . excuse the pun . . . kill two birds with one stone.'

'So we're just as much in danger from those countries,' said Angela.

'Not just those, Angela. Russia has interests in the region. The Americans might use any excuse to get a foothold in that same region, and a weapon of mass destruction is just the sort of thing that whets their appetite for war.'

'But they'd have to get permission from the other countries to fly in their airspace, yes?'

'They'll no doubt be working on that as we speak. The United Nations will become involved too. They'll debate whether a couple of dozen deaths on one train is a reasonable price to pay to stop countless deaths if the nuclear warhead goes off.' He sat on the bed opposite Angela and reached over to take her hands in his. 'In a few hours, the only ones looking out for the people on this train will be us.'

'Maybe . . . ' Angela stammered, as tears filled her eyes and the enormity of their situation hit her. 'Maybe they're right though, Mike. Perhaps we will have to die to save other people.'

'Then if that happens, it should be up to us to make it happen. Not some warmongers in Washington or Moscow.'

Angela shivered. 'You mean like the passengers who brought that plane down on nine eleven, before it hit the White House.'

'Yes, exactly like that. If I can't defuse the bomb, then I'll find a way to make sure it causes the minimum damage.' Mike squeezed her hand tight and she could feel the turmoil within him. 'I need to get as many people off this train as possible before I do that.'

'We,' said Angela.

'What?'

'You said 'I need to get as many people off this train as possible'. I'm saying *we* need to get as many people off this train as possible.'

'It's the same thing.'

'No it isn't. You're taking it all upon yourself, Mike. I could see you doing that in the restaurant car. But I won't let you take all the responsibility on your shoulders. I'm with you all the way. You don't have to do this alone.'

'I'll remind you of that when you're angry with me later.'

'Angry about what?'

He did not answer, but Angela could see the way his mind was working. Despite her own fears, she intended to prove to him that she could be just as determined as he was. She reached over and kissed his cheek lightly, hiding the fear that was steadily building inside her. 'Whatever happens, whatever choice you make, I want you to know that I forgive you.'

'You might,' said Mike, darkly. 'But I'm not sure if God will.'

'Well,' said Angela, slowly, trying to be tactful for Mike's sake. 'He is not here, but we are. So any choices we make are our concern.'

'Even if one of those choices involve killing everyone on this train?'

6

At lunch time, the passengers were taken back to the restaurant car and given sandwiches and cold drinks. Angela had to quickly put Mike back in handcuffs when they heard someone outside their cabin door. But at least they knew that she could get him free if necessary. At some point he would have to find a way out of their cabin. Until then, they decided to do as they were told so as not to raise any suspicions amongst the terrorists.

Once in the restaurant car, Mike realised that there were far more people working for Karloff than he had originally thought. As well as the two gunmen, Cal and Ambroise (who seemed to be working under duress) there were about a dozen other men. They looked as if they had been recruited from 'Hire-a-Thug'. They took up stations at either end of each of the four sleeping carriages, which used up eight of them. Some of the others guarded the buffet and the restaurant car, and Mike guessed others were at different vantage points on the train, perhaps near to the engine and the kitchen, which was in its own carriage, to the side of a long thin corridor between the eating areas and the sleeping quarters, and next door to the communal bathrooms.

Mike guessed the men were mercenaries rather than activists. They spoke several different languages between them and were of different ethnicities. As he ate a mozzarella cheese and tomato baguette, and sipped unpleasantly warm cola, he tried to work out what their weaknesses might be. He figured that it would be their lack of conviction for Karloff's cause. They were merely soldiers for hire, and would have no political inclinations. It meant that they would run before risking their lives on a train loaded with a dirty bomb. All Mike needed to work out was what might make them run even quicker.

When he had finished sizing up the bad guys, he turned to the passengers. There were ten women, twelve men, including himself and Angela, and the child. Two of the passengers Mike knew as Liberty and Harry, and there was one who looked like a rock star, but Mike could not place him.

The little boy had been brought to the restaurant car too and was eating a sausage roll and drinking milk. The woman, who Mike assumed was his mother, sat scowling at him. What sort of woman brought her child on a train that she knew could explode at any minute?

'Take him back to the cabin,' said Karloff.

'I'm sick of taking care of him,' said the girl.

'Do as I say, Patty.'

'Oy,' said Cal, stepping up to Karloff. 'Leave her alone.'

To Mike's amazement, Karloff backed down.

'I will take him,' said Ambroise, reaching for the child.

'Yeah, like we'd let that happen,' said Cal. 'I suppose I'll have to take him.'

'If it's that much trouble for you all, I'll look after him,' Angela said. She scowled at Patty. 'Some mother you are, bringing your child here at a time like this. Why would you do such a thing?'

'This child,' said Patty, scowling back at Angela, 'is our meal ticket.'

'Shut up, Patty,' said Cal, speaking even more savagely than Karloff had earlier. 'There's no need to give it all away.'

'Sorry,' she said, her eyes turning to granite. Mike suspected that Cal might pay for his outburst later, when his girlfriend had decided how to punish him. 'I just . . .'

'You just need to keep your mouth shut,' said Cal. 'Until we know for certain that this lot are dead, you say nothing. Right?'

112

'Yes, of course.'

Mike and Angela exchanged glances as Karloff, Cal, Patty and the little boy left the restaurant car. The mercenaries remained, but they did not seem too interested in the passengers, beyond blocking their way from the restaurant car.

'I think we should all introduce ourselves,' said Mike. 'It might be important if some of us get out of here. I'm Michael Fairfax and I'm a vicar from Stony End. I don't mind being called Mike. I have a son called Jamie. If anyone gets out I'd like him to know I love him.'

Angela swallowed hard, clearly moved. 'I'm Angela Cunningham. I'm an actress from Midchester. My dad is a retired vicar and my mum is a retired teacher. I'd like them to know I love them too.' She turned to Liberty. 'Liberty?' She spoke kindly enough, but Liberty frowned.

'My name is Liberty Cathcart and I'm from Stony End. This is my husband Harry.'

'Is that all?' asked Angela.

'If you want overly-emotional declarations of love for absent relatives, I'm afraid it is,' said Liberty.

Mike quietly fumed. Liberty's attitude made it harder for others to say what they wanted to say, because she had left them feeling self-conscious.

'I'm Will,' said the young porter, bravely when it was silent for too long. Mike wanted to shake his hand but as he was handcuffed he just smiled and nodded his encouragement. 'I'm a porter on this railway, and I was supposed to be going to university to study engineering. I haven't got anyone to send love to. I was brought up in a children's home.'

'No girlfriend?' asked Angela, gently. 'Or boyfriend?'

Will grinned. 'Nah, neither, and it would be a girl, in case anyone is wondering. Not that I'd really choose a few hours before I died to come out.'

That lightened the mood a little. A

few more passengers spoke up. One couple were from Paris and another were Americans, on their first trip to Europe. They gave a whole list of relatives to inform.

'Could you narrow it to just a couple?' Angela asked, kindly. 'I'm not sure we can remember all those names.'

'Well, I guess my sister Cora should know,' said the woman, reluctantly. 'She can tell the rest of the family.'

The majority were Russians who did not speak English, so the English passengers waited patiently whilst they shared information with each other. Then they reached the ageing rocker, who was travelling alone.

'I'm Jon Bliss,' he said. 'I was a big star in the nineties. I was on my way to Cariastan to play at a little club on the seafront. I'm not big in Japan anymore but I am big in Cariastan.'

'I remember you,' said Angela. 'Weren't you in that group with the odd name? Oh what was it?'

'The Joy of Sex Pocket Edition,' said

Jon. 'We had one hit, then I went solo and had another hit.'

'Is there anyone waiting at home for you, Jon?' asked Mike, shortly, feeling a little bit jealous about how much interest Angela seemed to be taking in Jon Bliss.

'Nah, no one. In fact . . . Oh it doesn't matter now. I wouldn't want to claim him anyway.'

'Who?' asked Angela.

'I had a letter from someone saying that boy Cal was my son from a one night stand I had in the late eighties. Well I think it's him, with the blond hair and everything. They just said it was some lad who worked on this train. That's why I decided to come by train instead of flying over. Stupid me, huh?'

No one knew how to answer that. A few more passengers spoke, and Mike did his best to remember them all. He hoped others would too.

He need not have worried. When they were taken back to the cabin,

Angela insisted on writing down everything they had been told. She took a notepad from her handbag, and started making the list, resting on the tiny table in the cabin.

'Mind you,' she said. 'They'll have a passenger manifest, won't they?'

'Yes, but that won't pass on the personal messages,' said Mike, undoing the handcuffs with the pin. He was dismayed to find he was not nearly as good at it as Angela. She cast him a sympathetic glance and took the clip off him.

'I told you you'd need me to help you,' she said, kissing him on the forehead like a mother with a helpless child. He was surprised to find he did not mind the feeling. It was nice to have someone to care for him. He had not known that comfort since his wife died.

'Now I need to find a way to get out of this cabin,' he said.

'I? Didn't I tell you it was 'we' from now on?'

'We then.' Mike stood up and looked

117

at the ceiling. There was a tiny skylight in the bathroom but there was no way he could fit through that. The window was sealed, and made from toughened safety glass, so it would be difficult to break it, even if he had some sort of tool with which to do it.

'It makes me wonder how they get people out if the train crashes,' he said.

'Maybe it's easy to remove from the outside,' Angela suggested. 'But they'll have cutting equipment anyway, won't they? The jaws of life or whatever they call them.'

'Yes, that's something we're sadly lacking.'

'That's men for you,' said Angela, wryly. 'Never prepared, even if they've been in the boy scouts. Girl Guides were much better.'

'Oh, so you happen to have a welding kit in your luggage, do you? Don't tell me, it's hidden in your lipstick.'

'Don't be silly. The lipstick is poisonous.' She blew him a kiss and he could not help but laugh.

Mike tried the door. He might be able to break it open, but that would make a lot of noise and alert the terrorists to what he was doing. They really were trapped.

'Put the handcuff back on again but don't lock it,' said Angela, when all other options had been exhausted.

'Why?'

'You're about to witness an Oscar winning performance. Just be ready. Oh I presume you're not averse to hitting someone, you being a vicar and all that.'

'I'll just add it to the reasons St Peter won't let me through the pearly gates,' Mike replied, sitting on the bunk and putting the cuff around his wrist.

'Don't worry,' said Angela, patting him on the head. 'It'll be much more fun where I'm going.'

'In that case, I can hardly wait.' She took a deep breath and shook her arms out, ready for her performance. 'Of course, this all relies on them only sending one gunman to deal with this.

Have you decided where you're going if this works?'

'I've got an idea.'

'I was afraid you were going to say that,' said Angela, looking up at the ceiling. 'Oh!' She screamed. It was so sudden and loud, that even Mike jumped. 'Oh, help. Ahhhh . . . ' She doubled up and squeezed tears into her eyes. 'Please, I need help. I feel ill.' She stuck her fingers down her throat and started to retch. That really brought the tears to her eyes.

A few moments later the cabin door opened and one of the mercenaries appeared. By that time, Angela was genuinely being sick. 'Help,' she croaked. 'I'm . . . Arggghhh.' Her groans were followed by another bout of retching. 'I need a doctor.'

'Come on,' said the mercenary, taking her arm, and spinning her around to escort her from the cabin. As he did so, Mike jumped up and brought both his fists down hard on the back of the man's head. It seemed the guy was even tougher than he looked. He only staggered slightly, but it was enough to make him loosen his grip on the machine gun. Mike grabbed it and pointed it straight at the man. Meanwhile Angela quickly shut the cabin door.

'Sit,' Mike said. 'One word and I shoot.' He handcuffed the man to the bed, making sure both hands were in the cuffs and above the man's head. It would be hard even for a man of his size to escape.

Angela went into her overnight case and took out a couple of scarves. She wrapped one around the man's mouth and another around his feet.

Mike opened the cabin door and stuck his head out. 'All clear,' he whispered to Angela. 'I'll come back for you. Okay?'

She nodded. 'I'm not exactly happy about it, but I know I'll only hold you up.

'Shut the window after me,' he said. 'And keep big boy there quiet for as long as you can.' The windows in the corridor did open, so Mike pulled one down and climbed out through it.

*   *   *

Angela could see the wind and the movement of the train buffeting him about and for one awful moment she thought he was going to fall. But he managed to hold on with the machine gun strapped over his back. She saw him hoist his body upwards. First his torso, then his legs disappeared up toward the top of the train. Slamming the window shut, she looked around and on seeing no one nearby — she assumed that the other gunman must have stepped out for a minute or two — she went back into the cabin and shut the door, falling against it before realising she could not show the man handcuffed to the bed any weakness.

Standing up straight, Angela glared at him. 'Now,' she said. 'Are you going to be good?'

He laughed through his gag, and tried to say something. Angela realised after a few minutes that he was pointing out that she did not have a weapon. 'Maybe not,' she said, reaching into her overnight case and taking out her manicure set. 'But I have a very nasty pair of nail clippers and a metal nail file.' She waved the nail file toward his eyes and was gratified to see that he shut up. She was obviously better at playing the *femme fatale* than she thought.

It was just five minutes before they came looking for the gunman. Karloff kicked the door open and had Angela manhandled and taken to the restaurant car. When she heard a shot whilst on the way to the restaurant car, she thought for one awful moment they had found Mike. She looked back and saw them carrying the guy Angela and Mike had imprisoned out of the cabin. They opened the door to the outside and threw him out. She felt bad about it, but only slightly. The man would have shot innocent people, if Karloff had ordered him to. He did not deserve her sympathy. Still, it did not make her feel good to know that she might have been the reason for his death. Promising herself a really nice nervous breakdown when the trip was over, she filed the guilt away for a more appropriate time.

'Where is your companion?' Karloff asked Angela, as one of the other gunmen shoved her into a booth in the restaurant car. She rubbed her upper arm, sure that he would have left a bruise or two.

'I have no idea.'

Karloff caught her by the hair and pulled hard. 'Where is he?'

'I said, I have no idea, and that's the truth.' She started to cry. 'I thought he was going to help us, but he just left me and jumped off the train. He could be dead or alive. I don't know. He let me down.' She sobbed bitterly, like a woman scorned. 'I thought he cared about me, but he just took off leaving me alone to deal with your man.'

'So not so brave, this man who was in the bomb squad, huh?'

'No,' said Angela, miserably. Karloff went up to the top of the restaurant car with his men. She guessed that he would search the train anyway. The sharp way he kept glancing at her suggested that she may not have convinced him about Mike jumping off the train.

Not that her tears had been fake. The idea of Mike out there, on his own, terrified her. One thing the little escapade had proved was that Karloff was reluctant to kill any of the passengers. The men who let him down, yes. But not the hostages.

She wondered why that was. It might have been because it had more impact if all the passengers were alive when the bomb went off. Or more likely Karloff hoped for a lighter sentence if he was caught. There was one other possibility, and the one that had occurred to Angela from the very beginning. Karloff was not in charge here. He dare not kill any passengers without the say so of whoever had arranged all this.

Nuclear weapons cost a lot of money, so whoever was backing the hijack must have access to that money. Russian gangsters perhaps? But what did they care about a small country like Cariastan becoming a monarchy again? Angela tried to remember what else she knew about the country, apart from what she had read in the newspaper article cum advertisement. It was very little. Like any country with the suffix 'stan' it became lost in a sea of similar sounding countries in Eastern Europe and the Middle East where there always seemed to be some sort of conflict. But Cariastan was not like that. Once the Russians had left, the people were pretty much united in their wish to become a monarchy again, and there had been none of the usual religious conflict that had marred so many of the countries which became free from Soviet control. Religions existed along-side each other quite happily in

Cariastan. Only the politicians who enjoyed their own power too much halted the return of the monarchy for years until a new generation came along and brought it about by peaceful means.

There was something else that Angela had heard, only the memory would not come to her. As she pondered, Ambroise approached the table and handed her a can of cola. They locked eyes and Angela felt for a moment that he was trying to impart something to her. Could she trust this man? In that moment she felt that she could.

'What does Cariastan have that anyone would want?' she asked quietly.

'Oil,' he said, before turning away quickly.

Of course! That was it. Oil had recently been found in Cariastan. That's what Karloff's boss wanted. But how would stopping the coronation bring that about? Surely the future king would only postpone the coronation.

'Could I have a sandwich, please?' she asked Ambroise. 'Being held hostage doesn't half make a girl feel hungry.'

He half turned and nodded. He went behind the bar and found a sandwich in the chiller, bringing it to Angela.

'How?' she asked in a low voice.

'Put another king in his place,' he murmured. 'One over whom they have complete control.'

'How could they do that?'

Ambroise was about to speak but Karloff seemed to have noticed they were talking. 'What is the actress saying?'

'She thinks I have poisoned her sandwich,' said Ambroise, swiping it from Angela's hand roughly. 'These actresses. They are so dramatic. Here,' he said, taking a bite from the sandwich. He chewed it then swallowed. 'It is safe, see?' He dropped the sandwich on the table and went back to Karloff.

Angela sat back in her seat, ignoring the sandwich, which she had not really wanted anyway. Her stomach was too churned up to eat anything.

How could they replace the king? And how would blowing up Cariastan help anyone get hold of the oil? It would turn the country, and everything around it, into a wasteland like Chernobyl where no one dare go for years and years.

So were the instigators of the terrorist act hoping that the current king would go for the lesser of two evils? He might allow someone else to sit in his place, rather than risk lives. Even so, everyone would know how that came about and the new king — or queen — would not be in power very long before the United Nations became involved and called for his abdication. No one wanted a leader who had been not only shown to have nuclear capabilities but the willingness to use them. Unless it was in the interests of some countries to keep him there because of the oil.

She wondered what sort of man would do such a thing.

7

Vicky Summers watched the television with growing horror, as did everyone else in the office. The presenter said that details were sketchy but that there had been reports that a train travelling from Nice to Cariastan had been hijacked and that King Henri was aware of the situation and would update the country when he had more details. The live stream of the train, taken from a helicopter, appeared on the screen. The presenter informed them that it would soon leave Austria and cross the border. However, there were further reports that the authorities over that border might refuse the train access into their country. How they intended to stop the train was not explained.

'I . . . I have to go,' she stammered to one of her workmates. She did not wait for a reply. She left the office, knocking things over in her urgency to get out. The First National Bank of Cariastan towered over her head like a mountain of glass, as she searched the street for a taxi. It occurred to her that she should have told her father where she was going, but there was no time for that. She would telephone him later, when he returned from his game of golf. He would no doubt see the news and understand her urgency.

When a taxi finally stopped, she ordered it to take her to the Summer Palace. She did not even know if King Henri was there, but it was as good a place to start as anywhere. Someone would know where to find him. As everyone else was heading out of the country, Vicky had only persuaded the taxi driver to take her to the palace by offering him triple the fare plus a large tip. He grunted and nodded, before switching on the meter and setting off.

'No tourists allowed inside,' said the Greek taxi driver in broken English. 'It is closed for coronation.'

131

'I don't care,' said Vicky. 'I have to go there. It's an emergency.'

The taxi ride seemed to take forever, even though Cariastan's capital was only small. The city was full to the brim with tourists, both from the outer provinces of Cariastan and from other countries. They had all come for the coronation. The bunting being put up on lampposts by men in cherry pickers gave the city a party atmosphere that Vicky did not feel.

She was not the only one who had lost the party spirit. Their progress to the palace was impeded by the number of people, both tourists and residents, now wanting to get out of Cariastan. Vicky saw people come out of their houses with all the worldly belongings they could possibly carry. Children were crying and fractious parents were struggling to calm them down.

It took the taxi an hour to make what was usually a ten minute journey.

Finally the taxi arrived at the Summer Palace, which stood on a rocky peninsular overlooking the sea. As the road was closed to all but official traffic at the bottom of the peninsular, Vicky had to walk the rest of the way, along a winding footpath, to a set of electronic iron gates, flanked by an eight foot wall. As soon as Vicky reached the gates, a guard wearing the white and gold ceremonial uniform of the Cariastan Army stepped forward to halt her progress.

'I need to see King Henri,' said Vicky. 'It's very important.'

'I am sorry, Miss,' said the guard. 'But His Royal Highness is not receiving visitors today.'

'No, you don't understand. I must see him. It's about the train that's been hijacked.' Vicky started to cry, which was not her intention. She had wanted to appear calm and collected. But now, with the King so near yet so far away from her, she began to realise the situation she was in. What if he did not believe her? There was no reason why he should. She did not have proof. At least not with her. 'I have information about the train that has been hijacked,' she said, more firmly. 'I know . . . ' she paused, not wanting to share her secret with the guard. 'I know some of the people on there, and it may be relevant to what's going on.'

'I'm sorry, Miss.'

'Please, tell King Henri that I knew his brother, Philipe!'

The guard looked at her for a moment, clearly thinking she was a mad woman. But he also looked a bit out of his depth. He was very young after all. Probably younger than Vicky, who was twenty-four.

'I will fetch someone.'

Vicky waited agonising minutes whilst the soldier disappeared inside the palace. His place was taken by another guard, who kept glancing at her quizzically. He had probably overheard her outburst and was planning to shoot her if she so much as stepped out of line. She curbed her natural desire to see the king and tried to calm down so she would not appear to be a threat.

It was nearly half an hour before the guard returned with another man. He was very good looking, probably in his thirties, but with a savage, hawk-like face.

'You wanted to see the king?' he asked.

'Yes,' said Vicky, quailing under the man's suspicious gaze. He was not dressed in uniform, yet he was more frightening than the guards. 'I have important information about the train, and the people on it.'

'Yes, this is what the guard said.' The man became amiable, speaking as one might speak to someone with learning difficulties. 'Tell me what this information is, and I'll pass it onto the King.'

The man's sudden change of tone alerted Vicky to what was going to happen next. Two men appeared from nowhere and caught her by the arms. 'Take her to the guardhouse,' said the hawk-like man. 'Find out what she knows.'

'No, you don't understand,' said Vicky, pushing the men off. 'I'm not in on it. You have to help me. Please.' She began to cry again, and hated herself for it, but the pressure of being brave, even for only an hour, was too much. 'My little boy is on that train. My nanny was supposed to be bringing him to me in Cariastan, because I work at the bank here now and I wanted him with me.' The words poured out, and she knew that what she said sounded incoherent, but she had to make the hawk-like man understand. 'She said she doesn't like flying so she was bringing him on the train. I thought he would love that. He loves trains, you see. Especially Thomas the Tank Engine. I thought he'd love sleeping on a train. I should have come with him really. I would have loved to share the experience with him, but I had to work. Only now I don't think that's why she did it. The nanny, I mean. I think she means to hurt him or use him to hurt others and you have to help me to get him back.'

'I am sorry about your child,' said the man, in gentler tones. 'But we are doing all we can to help the passengers. Of course, any information you have about them will be helpful to us so if you would come to the guard room. You're not under arrest, of course . . . '

'No, you don't understand. My little boy. My Solomon . . . ' She almost crumbled completely then, saying her baby's name out loud and thinking of the awful danger he was in. 'He's the son of Prince Philipe.'

* * *

Anton was with his Director of Security, looking over the pictures of passengers from the train, when Faust brought the girl to him.

'This is Vicky Summers,' said Faust. 'She says she's the mother of your nephew.'

Anton could not help being surprised both by her sudden appearance in the palace and the way she looked. She was much younger than he had expected. His brother had been forty when he died, but the girl was clearly in her early to mid-twenties. She was also much fresher looking than he had imagined. Philipe had been drawn to girls who were a bit on the free and easy side.

With her blonde hair tied up in a tight bun, and her clear, make-up free face, Anton could see that Vicky Summers was lovely — even with her eyes full of tears — but he could not see what drew his playboy brother to her.

'Please, Miss Summers, sit down,' said Anton, gallantly. Faust drew a chair up from the side of the study and Vicky sat down unsteadily. Anton could tell from his friend's face that Faust did not trust the girl or her motives. But it would not hurt to treat her courteously until they found out the truth. 'Would you like anything? Tea? Coffee?'

'A cup of tea would be nice, please,' Vicky hiccoughed through her tears. 'You must believe I had nothing to do with this,' she carried on frantically. 'I only wanted my little boy near to me in Cariastan because I missed him so much.'

She began to sob. Anton took a tissue from a box on the desk and gave it to her. 'What do you know about what's happened?' Faust asked.

'I told you, I know nothing. Only that Patty, my nanny, was bringing him to me on the train because she said she did not like flying. I thought he would be fine, because my brother, Cal, works on the same train and he promised to look out for them both.'

'Your brother?' Anton went back to the desk and picked up a picture of a good looking young blond man. 'This is your brother?'

'Yes. Cal Summers. Oh God, what if she's hurt them both?'

'I don't think Patty is alone in this,' said Anton. He and Faust exchanged glances. Pictures taken from a helicopter flying over the train had appeared to show that Cal Summers, unlike the rest of the passengers and crew, had complete freedom to move around. Another picture, that Anton had not shown Vicky, was of Cal with a machine gun in his hands. 'She may have others on the train working with her. From what we know of her, she works for an organisation called Belladonna. She's an assassin, but also turns her hand to industrial espionage, and as we realise now, kidnapping. The person who has been sending us messages is called Karloff. Do you know that name?'

Vicky shook her head. 'No, I'm sorry. I've never heard of anyone of that name. Well, except Boris Karloff, of course. What are they threatening? Are they saying they're going to hurt Solomon? Is that it? My father is very rich. He runs The First National Bank of Cariastan, and other banks throughout the world. He could pay them

140

anything they wanted. I just want my baby back.'

'That isn't what they want,' said Anton. 'What they want is for me to step down as King. And whilst we don't know this for certain yet, we think that they want to put Solomon in my place.'

'No!' said Vicky. 'They can't. He's just a baby.'

'He's also not . . . ' Anton paused. 'I'm sorry to be rude, but he can't accede to the throne anyway, as you and my brother weren't married.'

'Oh . . . ' Vicky looked down at the floor. Anton felt sure she was going to say something else, but instead she clamped her mouth shut. 'Of course, I understand,' she said after a moment's pause.

'Tell me how you met my brother,' he said. He pulled up another chair and sat opposite her, feeling that to have him and Faust towering over her might intimidate the girl too much.

'I was working as a croupier in Las Vegas one summer whilst on break from university,' she said. 'My dad wasn't very pleased, but at the time I wasn't ready to go into the family business. I wanted to see the world. Philipe was there with friends and he kept coming to my table. I thought he was very dashing and handsome.' She smiled. 'I suppose I allowed myself to be seduced.' There was a long pause, and Anton suspected she was leaving a lot out, but he had no idea what. 'Then I went home and found out I was pregnant. I was about to contact Philipe and tell him about the baby when his security guard, who knew about us, came to tell me that Philipe had died.'

'Didn't you think to tell the rest of Philipe's family?' asked Faust.

'Not really. To be honest, I wasn't sure how I would be received. And it's not as if I needed money.'

'But you must understand that I would have liked to know about my nephew,' said Anton, with only a hint of reproach in his voice.

'Yes, I can see that now. I'm sorry. But I honestly didn't want anything and I suppose I didn't want you to think I was after something. I know about Philipe's reputation. He was very honest with me. I imagined there might be lots of girls with a claim on him and I didn't want to be one of them. I did love him, you know. Now I just want my little boy back so I can take him home and look after him. I never wanted him to be a prince. I just want him to grow up as a normal, happy little boy.'

'Anything you can tell us about Patty would be helpful,' said Anton. He picked up a picture from the desk. 'First of all, can you confirm this is her?' He held the picture up for Vicky to see.

She nodded. 'Yes, that's her. Patricia Newman. She came with good references. She used to work for one of my father's friends, and they were very happy with her. She's not the most cheerful of women, but she seems to

like Solomon and he just loves every-
body. She's looked after him for six
months now and I never had any reason
to doubt her.'

'And your brother, Cal. This is him,
yes?' Anton held up another picture.

'Yes, that's Cal.'

'If I show you more pictures, can you
tell me if you know any of the people?'

'Yes, of course. I'm happy to help if I
can. Anything to get Solomon home
safely.'

'Very well,' said Anton. He held up
an enlarged passport photograph of a
good looking man in his fifties. 'Have
you ever seen this man?'

Vicky shook her head. 'I'm sorry, no I
don't know him . . . oh hang on a
minute. He does look a bit familiar.
Wasn't he that vicar who went mad at
that memorial service a while back?'

Anton frowned. 'It does say his name
is Reverend Michael Fairfax. What
about this woman? She and the
reverend seem to be together.' He did
not explain how he knew that as he did

not want to alert Vicky to the fact that they had taken pictures from outside the train. He held up a picture of Angela Cunningham.

'Oh everyone knows her,' said Vicky. 'It's Pandora.'

Anton frowned. 'It says here that her name is Angela Cunningham.'

'She's an actress,' Vicky explained. 'She was in *Pandora's Vox*. I suppose you didn't get that in Cariastan during the Soviet era.'

'No, I don't think we did, but I lived in Paris then anyway. I don't think they showed it there either.' Anton went through several more of the pictures. Vicky knew the young black man called William.

'That's Will,' she said. 'In fact, he's the reason that Cal went to work on the train. Will got a job on it, and then Cal followed him. Will's a bit of a geek, and loves old films, but he's a lovely lad.' Anton sensed she was telling the truth when she said she did not know any of the other passengers. Finally he showed her the picture of Ambroise.

'Do you know this man?' he asked. 'His name is . . . '

'Vincent Ambroise,' said Vicky, standing up suddenly. 'Don't you know him?'

'No, why would I?'

'Surely you know him. He's . . . he was Philipe's bodyguard. The one who told me about Philipe's death. He is also Solomon's godfather. Oh no . . . ' Vicky put her hands to her face. 'Please, don't tell me that he's in on this. I thought he was my friend . . . '

'We're not sure what his role is,' said Anton, honestly. 'He seems to be doing what Karloff tells him, but he doesn't seem to do so willingly.'

'How do you know this?' asked Vicky. 'Have you spies on the train?'

'No, but we have had helicopters taking pictures and filming through the windows,' Anton admitted.

'So you can see if Solomon is alright?'

'As far as we know, he is being treated well, though we did not know until you came here whether he was definitely my nephew. There are no other children on the train that we could see, but that did not mean they were not there. But then again we didn't know if my brother's child was in his teens. It was a possibility.' All Anton had ever known was that his brother fathered a child. No one had known where or when.

Before Vicky could respond, the telephone rang. At Anton's behest, the Minister for Defence answered it. He spoke a few words in Greek, and then put the phone down.

'We have more news on the reverend,' he said, gravely.

'What is it?' asked Anton.

The director of security looked at Vicky, seeming to hesitate. 'He used to be in the British army. In the bomb squad to be more precise.'

'So he could be in on it,' said Anton, frowning.

'What have bombs got to do with anything?' asked Vicky, her face turning pale. 'Tell me, please.'

'The terrorists are claiming that the train has a nuclear device attached to it that will be detonated when they arrive in Cariastan at midnight.'

If Anton had any doubts as to Vicky's innocence before then, her reaction to the news about the bomb proved it beyond reasonable doubt. She crumbled to the floor sobbing, 'Oh my baby. My baby.'

* * *

Vicky woke up some time later, lying in a luxurious bed. She had been given a sedative. Faust di Luca sat at her bedside with his arms folded. He got up and helped her to sip a glass of water, then sat back down and folded his arms again.

'You don't trust me, do you?' she said, when she had recovered a little.

'I don't trust anyone with the power to hurt my best friend. I also think there's still something you're not telling us.'

'All I want . . .'

148

'Yes, yes,' said Faust. 'All you want is your little boy back safe. But how much better would it be for you if he could be king of Cariastan, especially now we've found oil?'

'I don't need money. My father is probably richer than your king. I don't care about oil either.'

'What about power? Whoever controls the little boy, if the terrorist's plan works, controls the throne.'

'If I cared about power I would have . . . ' Vicky stopped suddenly. 'I don't care about power and if you think I'm the sort of person who would use my proximity to the throne to gain power then perhaps you're judging me by your own standards. Philipe told me all about you. How you latched onto his brother when you were both at university.'

'Philipe didn't like me because I didn't like him. I felt he was bringing the name of the Cariastan royal family into disrepute with his playboy antics. Hiring body guards who had not been properly screened was one of the many headaches he caused. He just picked people he liked, regardless of their back ground. Philipe was reckless and thoughtless.'

'Philipe was not like that. At least not with me.'

'Then you must be a remarkable woman.'

'No, I'm just ordinary and perhaps that's what he needed at the time. Maybe that's why he hired Ambroise. Because he hadn't been vetted and approved by the family. Look, Mr. di Luca, I don't know what else I can say to convince you that I have nothing to do with any of this. If you're so sure, have me arrested. All I ask is that even if I am arrested, you see that my little boy gets home safe to my family.' A tear ran down her cheek. Tired of fighting, Vicky lay down and hid her head in the pillow.

She heard a voice from the door ask for Faust di Luca, but she did not hear him leave.

'What is it?' asked Faust, entering the operations room that had been set up to deal with the incident. All the main branches of the armed and police services were represented in the people in the room. Many sat at consoles, deciphering information as it came in.

'Come and look at this. We've only just got these pictures through,' said Anton. 'They were filmed a while ago from a chopper. Since we received this, we've lost visual contact. We're trying to get it back now, but it may take a while.'

On a plasma screen, almost the size of a cinema screen, there was a film running of the train. A man sat on the roof of the train, firing bullets at the helicopter, almost playfully. Suddenly, from the far side of the train, another man appeared and proceeded to climb onto the roof of the train, settling flat on his stomach. Faust frowned. 'Is that . . . ?'

'The Fairfax guy,' said Anton. 'Now

why would he be getting out onto the roof of the train if he was with the terrorists?'

'Maybe he's a lookout.'

'I don't think so. There's one at the front of the train. It doesn't make sense to send another man out there. Anyway watch a bit longer, and you'll see that he's on our side. It's just unfortunate that things take a turn for the worst when they reach the border.'

Faust watched aghast as the train reached the barriers. There was no sound on the video, yet he could almost hear the sickening screech of metal and sense the terror of the passengers as the train hit the barriers and several tons of rolling stock buckled and broke in two.

8

When Mike left Angela behind he had managed to get onto the roof of the train. He found himself buffeted about by the helicopter overhead. It swooped down lower to him, but he waved it away. He could so easily have let it pick him up so as to escape from the situation, but there was no way he was leaving Angela or the others to their fate.

He thought about her, left alone with that gunman, and wished he had taken her with him. But he could hardly guarantee his own safety, let alone hers.

Lying flat on the top of the train, he looked around him, spinning on his stomach to get a three hundred and sixty degree view. At the far end, three carriages away from him, he could see a man with a machine gun, sitting on top of the car just before the engine. Mike mentally ticked off what he knew of the train's layout and realised that it was the restaurant car. So the bomb was either in the restaurant car, or the main engine. Mike guessed it was the main engine. Even if all the other carriages came adrift, the terrorists would want to make sure the bomb reached its target.

Every now and then the lookout half turned and lazily fired a volley of bullets toward the helicopter, but with no obvious thoughts of damaging it. The man was just posturing, and the helicopter pilot, who was probably some news guy out for an exclusive, seemed to enjoy the exchanges, swooping nearer to encourage more action. No doubt the viewers at home would be fascinated. For them it would be like watching a Bruce Willis film, and no one would really consider the real human cost of what was happening.

At least the helicopter was keeping the man's attention at the far end of the train, and away from Mike. He would like to give the pilot the benefit of the doubt, and believe that was what he was doing, but Mike knew from personal experience that the media were more interested in getting a story, and it was a better story if or when someone died.

He crawled along the train, hoping that the helicopter would continue to keep the man looking the other way, but unfortunately it decided to film him too, just as he feared. It swooped back up the length of the train in his direction. Mike started to crawl toward the front of the train and just managed to hurl himself into the gap between the two carriages before the man with the gun followed the line of the chopper.

When the helicopter came abreast of Mike, he gestured, quite obscenely, for it to get away from him. He hoped there were no children watching at home, but at least it seemed to work. The helicopter moved upwards again and went back to the front of the train. However, when he peeked out from the side, he could see that it was pointed in his direction. He had been right. The story the cameraman filmed for the viewers at home was more important than the lives of those on the train.

He pulled himself back in between the carriages and planned how he could get past the guard on top and then to the front of the train. He dare not go back on the roof, with the helicopter pilot determined to draw attention to him every few minutes. He might be able to get along the side of the train. He figured the corridor side would be best. There might be less chance of him being seen, but he would have to be careful with the guards at each end of the carriages.

He reached around the side of the train and found a strip of metal piping to hold onto. It wasn't perfect, but there was a board at the bottom of the carriage that engineers and cleaners used to reach the top of the carriage. He stood on that and clung to the side of the train, next to a window, taking stock of what was around him.

At each end of every carriage was a small metal maintenance ladder leading to the roof. Mike wished he had known about that when he hauled himself from the window! Still, at least he knew how to get up there again if he needed to. He waited for several minutes, and heard the commotion when Angela was taken to the restaurant. He breathed a sigh of relief. At least she was still alive. He saw them throw the dead man from the train on his side, and like Angela felt guilty. Like her, he put it aside for later. There was no time for regrets now. The man had made his choice and it had involved the possible deaths of all the passengers and many of the people of Cariastan.

He was about to move again a little while later when someone opened the window next to him. 'The child needs fresh air,' he heard Ambroise say. He could hear the little boy whimpering.

'The child needs to shut up and go to sleep,' Patty said. If Mike had thought she was the boy's mother, her harsh words told him otherwise. 'I'll give him something.'

'No' said Ambroise. 'No more. You will not damage the child with more drugs.'

'You don't give the orders, Ambroise,' said Patty. 'You take them. That's the deal. You do as we say or your little prince here gets it.'

'Then all your efforts will be wasted,' said Ambroise. 'You think I do not know this? You think I don't know that you dare not hurt him for real? If you kill him, then all your plans will be for nothing. I do not think your boss will be very happy either.'

Mike could not see Patty, but he sensed that she hesitated then. 'Oh you look after him for a while,' she said. 'You know better than to cross Karloff.'

'Karloff is not in charge here though, is he?' said Ambroise. 'It's the one you call The Handler. Still, leave the child with me. I'll take care of him.'

Mike heard Patty move away. Then he heard Ambroise say soothingly,

'Don't worry, little prince. I promised your mama and papa I would always take care of you, and I will.'

That was twice the child had been referred to as a little prince. It might be a term of endearment, if only Ambroise had said it, but Patty said it too, albeit in more disparaging tones. Whether Ambroise was the child's father or grandfather, Mike did not know, but he was linked to the child somehow, just as Mike and Angela had suspected. But he was doing the terrorists' bidding. Could that be just to keep the child safe?

After a while, Ambroise closed the window. Mike waited a few more minutes and then checked to see if the coast was clear. He moved gingerly along the train, afraid that a gust of wind or a sudden change of tracks might throw him off. There was very little movement in the corridor. All the hostages were locked in their rooms, and the gunmen, one at either end of each corridor, weren't looking for anything coming from the outside.

Slowly, agonisingly, Mike managed to get to the end of that carriage. He threw himself into the space between the carriages, clinging onto the ladder for dear life. 'I'm getting too old for this,' he muttered to himself. The next bit would be harder. He knew that Karloff had set up his command centre in the restaurant cars. The buffet car, with its vending machines and sandwich bar, was occupied by a couple of the gunmen who weren't on guard. As Mike moved back to the side of the train and peered through the window, he could see them playing cards and talking, whilst drinking beer from cans. Great, thought Mike, that's all we need: drunken terrorists. In his experience that usually led to people dying.

He was about to try and move a little way across the carriage when the train straightened and he got a good look at the border, which was still a few miles away. Although it was in the distance, he could see helicopters and planes flying overhead, and there seemed to be a mass of people waiting. He guessed they were soldiers. As he guessed, they were going to try and stop the train before it reached their borders.

Flinging himself back into the space between the carriages, he climbed the ladder to the roof, so he could get a better look. 'Oh God . . . ' he said, when he realised he was right. Forgetting about defusing the bomb and about being seen, Mike ran along the top of the train, jumping across the gaps between the carriages till he reached the gunman who was on lookout.

As if hearing the thump of Mike's feet on the roof, the man turned and jumped up, pointing the gun at Mike.

'You won't need to shoot me, if we get nearer to that lot,' said Mike, shouting above the roar of the engine. 'They're going to blow up the train. Look!' He pointed to the distance.

'Yeah,' the man called back. 'I'm not falling for that one.'

'Then you're a bigger idiot than I

161

thought,' said Mike. Suddenly the train lurched, throwing them both sideways. It was the advantage that Mike needed to get the man's gun. Once he had it, he used the butt end of it to hit the man, throwing him from the train and into some soft grass at the side of the train tracks. The man might break an arm or leg, but he would live, which was more than the rest of them would if Mike didn't do something soon.

He climbed down into the cabin of the engine, where the two drivers were looking ahead and talking frantically over a radio in Russian. 'If that's Karloff,' said Mike, taking them both by surprise, 'tell him he has to stop this train now. You understand?' He pointed to the buffers which were drawing ever nearer.

Even if they did not speak English, they understood the urgency of the situation. But whoever was on the end of the radio did not. Judging by their stricken expressions, they were being told not to stop.

Mike grabbed the radio. 'For God's sake, Karloff, show some sense in your life. If this train hits those buffers, we're all dead.'

A voice asked in broken English, 'Who is this? I demand to know.'

'I might ask the same question,' said Mike, 'but I really don't have time.' He threw the radio down, deciding to worry about the strange voice on the other end later. He had noted that the train drivers weren't armed. At least not with guns. He took the machine gun from his back and pointed it at them. 'Stop the train. Now. Or I'll kill you both.'

The two drivers looked at Mike, looked at the gun, looked at the mass of military vehicles waiting to shoot them down, and did something he did not expect. They jumped out of the other side of the cabin, and into the fields.

Mike looked helplessly at the controls. One of them had to be the brake, but he had no idea which one. So he just kept pressing buttons and pulling levers, until he found the one that slowed the train. But it might be too late. At the speed the train was going there was not enough stopping room before the border

As the border drew ever nearer, the soldiers started firing, and so did some of the helicopters up above, though they mostly kept to their own side, probably aware that to do so in Austrian territory might be considered an act of war. Mike felt a sharp tug at his arm, and was only vaguely aware of it, until he realised that blood was oozing out. He had been hit, but he did not have time for that and he could not stay out of sight. He had to stop the train. Who knew what might happen to the nuclear device if they blew up the train?

As the train moved nearer to the border, Mike saw that the military had other plans. Two sets of buffers had been set up on the track. They were going to try and crash the train and bring a halt to its progress that way.

* ★ *

'What's happening?' said Angela, as the sound of shooting filled the air. No one in the car had any idea of what had just happened with Mike and the train drivers.

'We're slowing down,' said Ambroise, who had come back to the restaurant car with Solomon. He was giving the little boy some food.

Karloff, who had been dozing in one of the booths near the door jumped up and ran to the window. 'We cannot be slowing down.'

'Yes we are,' said Angela.

Karloff snapped open his phone and hit what Angela could only assume was a speed dial number.

'We're slowing down,' he said to someone at the other end. He listened for a moment. 'No, I do not know if the drivers disobeyed your instructions. I did not even know what was happening.' Karloff went pale, as the person on the other end clearly gave him bad news. 'But surely . . . ' he tried to say. 'But sir . . . We will all die . . . and the boy? Yes sir, I understand the mission. But . . . ' He snapped the phone shut and went out of the door to the other buffet car.

Angela heard him giving instructions in Russian, and soon some of the gunmen were running through the main restaurant car and towards the engine. 'Kill them,' said Karloff. 'Kill them both.'

He glared at Angela. 'If your man has anything to do with this.'

'I hope he has,' she spat back. 'Whatever this is. Are you going to tell us?'

'The government of the next country have put buffers on the track, because they do not want this train going through their country. If we hit it, then it could be the end for all of us.'

Ambroise snatched up Solomon. 'Then he must leave the train,' he said.

'No,' said Karloff. 'The Handler says not. He says that the international condemnation will do what the bomb failed to do. It will bring down the Cariastan king.'

'You're going to let a little boy die for politics,' said Angela. 'What sort of man are you?'

'I thought that was obvious, Miss Cunningham.'

'Well yes, you've obviously kidnapped a child — a very important child — and have no compunction in blowing up a country. But somehow, Karloff, I don't think you imagined things would end like this. I think that you thought you were going to get off this train before anything bad happened.'

'That was the plan, yes,' said Karloff. 'And so would the child. But the plan has changed. The Handler is a man who . . . We don't have time for this,' said Karloff. He ran after the men he had sent to the engine.

It left Ambroise and Angela completely alone with Solomon, because all the other gunmen were in the buffet car, and had orders to only come to the restaurant car if Karloff called them.

'I must get him off the train,' said Ambroise.

'The train is slowing. If you jump with him now, you might not be badly hurt,' said Angela.

Ambroise nodded. 'I swore to protect him all his life. That is why I'm here.'

'Save the story for when we have more time,' said Angela, kindly. 'Here . . .' She took her chunky sweater off. 'Wrap this around him. It might help stop him being scratched too badly by the fall.'

There was a door at the end of the restaurant car. The train slowed even more as it started to go up an incline, until it was only moving at walking pace, and the hilly grass covered ground outside was very close. Angela instinctively knew Mike was responsible for the train slowing, even though she had no real reason to be sure. Karloff's men were all cowards, but Mike was not. She opened the door, and Ambroise positioned himself in the gap, holding Solomon wrapped tightly to him.

She felt a sudden lump in her throat, terrified for the safety of the little boy and the danger they were putting him in. She did not know why she should even trust Ambroise, yet there was something about the way he behaved with the child that told her he would die for the little boy if he had to. 'Promise me that you'll take him back to his mummy.'

Ambroise nodded. 'Yes, I will.'

'Go, now!'

The train was moving as slow as it was going to get without actually stopping, giving Angela hope that Ambroise and the little boy would be unharmed.

Ambroise jumped. All Angela saw was his dark clad figure rolling in the grass, then the train moved on towards the top of the incline, and both Ambroise and Solomon were lost to sight.

Things happened very quickly then.

There was a volley of shots coming from outside, pinging off the edge of the train, and some hitting the windows, which thankfully only cracked slightly. She threw herself to the floor, only narrowly missing being hit by a stray bullet. 'You should have jumped with Ambroise and Solomon,' she muttered to herself. But she knew that she would never leave Mike alone to deal with the danger, no matter how attractive escaping might seem at that moment.

Karloff's men started herding the other passengers into the restaurant car. Angela could only guess they had been ordered to do so. She shuddered, knowing that it meant they would be nearer to the engine and therefore take the full brunt of the crash. The idea filled her with horror, not least about the cold, vicious man behind this scheme who would allow such a thing to happen to innocent people, rather than give up his insane plot.

One of the men hoisted her up off

the floor and pushed her towards one of the seats.

'You seem to know everything,' said Liberty Cathcart, viciously, as she was manhandled into the seat on the opposite side of the aisle. 'What's happening?'

'We're going to crash,' said Angela. She decided to forgive Liberty for her unpleasantness. The woman was afraid and about to die. Maybe she had earned the right to be nasty. 'I'm sorry,' she added, gently.

Liberty sank into one of the chairs. 'No . . . that can't be right. People always get out of these things, don't they?'

'Maybe in films,' said Angela, miserably. 'But not in real life.'

* *. *

The border came ever closer. Mike had managed to slow the train so far, but the brake had stuck. He pushed with all his might to make it go that bit further, but to no avail. He could hear the wheels screeching on the tracks beneath him. It was like nails on a blackboard, setting his teeth on edge.

'Stop,' said a voice behind him.

'That's what I'm trying to do,' he said.

'No, stop. Stop stopping the train,' the gunman said, uncertainly.

He felt a gun at the back of his head. 'Do you really think I am afraid of you shooting me when we're about to hit that barrier?' asked Mike. 'Go ahead, because we're all going to die anyway.'

The gunmen looked up ahead. By then Mike was not too surprised when they did exactly what the engine drivers did. They jumped off the train! Karloff entered just as they left. He took one look at the situation and nodded.

He muttered an obscenity, then added 'Good luck, Reverend,' before following his men off the train.

Mike barely had time to be surprised by Karloff's defection. He was still trying to stop the train.

He pulled one last time at the brake lever, but it came off in his hand. They got to the top of the incline and as the train hit the decline it started to speed up, getting faster and faster, with plenty of time to hit the buffers on the border at a terrifying pace. The last thing he saw before he felt someone crack him on the head was a piece of buffer flying, almost in slow motion, across the engine window.

*   *   *

'Dear God . . . ' said Faust, watching in the control room. The train hit the buffers at tremendous speed. As it did so, the whole train buckled. The back carriages came off the tracks and flew into the air, disengaging from the engine and the restaurant car, and rolling into the fields around the tracks, over and over before coming to a juddering halt.

The engine and the restaurant car carried on, through the buffers, past the horrified soldiers, who were helpless to do anything to stop the horror, and over the border.

'Casualties?' said Faust, unable to articulate any further.

'We don't know,' Anton replied. 'The media helicopter had to move to a safe distance because that idiot was shooting at it. We're trying to get our own people in there. All we have are these shots you see. Some of the terrorists jumped out of the engine, and we're trying to round them up, but we don't know what was happening on the far side of the train.'

'Your nephew?'

Anton looked at his friend darkly, his face a mask of pain. 'I don't know, Faust. He could have been in any one of those carriages. Emergency services are there now, doing all they can. But you can imagine the debris they have to sift through. It will be hours before we know anything.'

'Meanwhile, we have a runaway train with a nuclear bomb on it,' said the Secretary of Defence in solemn tones.

'No one can stop it now. The only thing people can do is get out of the way. We're talking with the authorities in all the countries it will pass through so they can get their rolling stock out of the way. But it might not be possible. There could be worse to come yet.'

'That's if the passengers aren't all dead anyway,' said Anton.

'I hate to be the one to state the unpleasant truth,' said Faust, 'but if all the passengers are dead then we can try to stop the train, maybe even reroute it.'

'To go where?' said Anton. 'There is nowhere we can send it that isn't inhabited.' He shook his head, and swallowed hard. 'The evacuation of Cariastan has already begun, but I'd like you to make sure it continues smoothly, Faust. We have to get everyone out of the country as soon as possible. It's on its way to Cariastan, whether we like it or not. You must go too. I insist.'

'What about you?' asked Faust, already guessing the answer.

'I'm staying here to be with those who can't get out in time.'

'If you're staying, then I'm staying too,' said Faust.

'They'll need a leader, Faust. Someone who can keep them calm and stop anarchy ruling the streets. We've already heard rumours of looting.'

'There are enough generals in the Cariastan army who are experienced enough to deal with that. I won't run away and hide from a terrorist attack, Anton. Not when you're staying in the eye of the storm.'

'If I'm truly honest, I was hoping you would say that.' Anton shook his friend's hand. 'So we face whatever comes and show the terrorists that we won't be frightened away from our country.'

The two friends stood shoulder to shoulder, determined either to ride out the coming storm or die in it.

9

Karloff had gone, along with some of the gunmen. His place as leader was filled by Cal and Patty. This made Angela even more afraid. Karloff had been amiably evil, and it had clearly been an act. Cal was like a little boy playing at being a big frightening man. Patty was as cold as ice and Angela was reminded of the adage about the female of the species being more deadly than the male.

As she cradled an unconscious Mike in her lap, she watched Cal's expression. He had been fine when he could hide behind Karloff, but now the strain was showing.

'Where's the kid?' he snapped. 'Where is he?'

'Gone,' said Angela, stroking Mike's head.

'Gone? Where?' Cal glowered over

her, holding a machine gun aloft. Judging by the way he held it he had very little training. Angela was not an expert shooter, but she had to learn how to hold a gun in a way that was authentic. So she had taken lessons. There were strict safety rules about guns, and how one held them.

She guessed that Cal was not bothered about safety, or whether he shot anyone, but even so, he looked like an amateur. And that, in Angela's opinion, was a very dangerous thing. It meant that he could shoot at any time if his nerves got the better of him.

Patty was much more calm and collected, and seemed to know her way around a gun. Cal was dangerous because of his extreme nervousness. Patty was dangerous because of her extreme calm.

'Gone where?' Cal asked again.

'Ambroise jumped off the train with him, way back in Austria. They're probably on their way to a police station now.'

'Unless Karloff gets to them first,' said Cal with a cocky grin.

'Do you think Karloff is bothered about finishing this?' asked Angela. 'He's left you. He doesn't even know about Ambroise and the child.'

'They're probably dead anyway,' said Patty. 'Jumping from the train like that . . . Ambroise probably crushed the kid.'

Angela shuddered. That thought had not occurred to her. She sent up a silent prayer that Ambroise somehow fell without hurting the baby. But what if Ambroise himself was badly hurt? Dead even? Solomon would be all alone out there. She could only pray that whoever was dealing with the crash would spread the net wider and find both of them alive and well, even if they did have slight injuries from the jump.

'What do we do?' Cal asked Patty. 'What do we do now, Patty? My . . . the Handler will be furious with us for losing the kid.'

'He'll be even more furious that his

plan to make sure we all died failed,' said Angela, before Patty could reply. 'I mean that was the intention in bringing everyone up to this carriage, wasn't it? To make sure we were killed when the train hit the buffers? In fact the way I see it, you'd have died too.'

'Shut up!' Cal raised his hand and was about to slap Angela when Will jumped up and grabbed his hand.

'What are you doing, mate?' asked Will. 'All this,' he gestured around the carriage, 'and hitting a woman? What's happened to you?'

'Oh nothing's happened to me, Dorothy,' said Cal, derisively. 'You're an idiot, you know that? I found out everything I needed to know about this train after five minutes with you. It's thanks to your information about the schematics and what all the workers did that we were able to take it.'

'Then you're the idiot,' said Will, rolling his eyes heavenward. 'Everyone knows it's owned by the First Bank of Cariastan, and there are schematics of the train on the website, along with how many people work here and what their different roles are. You had to go and play secret agent and convince yourself you were working undercover. Well done on that. You learned from me what you could have learned if you'd just used Google. Or you could have just asked your dad.'

Cal glared at Will, but Will held his stare until the blond boy backed down and went to talk to Patty.

Will sat back down opposite Angela. 'Are you okay?' he asked her.

'Yes, thanks, Will.' She frowned a little. Something about what Cal had said to Will had struck a chord with her. He was just trying to make his friend feel bad, but there was more than that. 'What did you mean when you said Cal could have asked his dad?'

'He runs the First Bank of Cari-astan,' said Will. 'Amongst lots of other banks. Alexander Summers is a big name in the banking world. Well according to Cal he is. I'd never heard of him. It seems to me he's more a behind the scenes type of bloke.'

★ ★ ★

Alexander Summers returned to the bank after a morning playing golf, followed by a leisurely lunch, with a sheik of his acquaintance. At least that was what it said in his schedule.

Summers was a very handsome man in his fifties, with carefully manicured nails. He was wearing a suit that would cost a year's wages for most people. He could have passed for a diplomat, or even a minor royal. He liked to tell people that his family were from the same line as the Mountbattens. In reality he had started his life as a clerk in a provincial bank, the son of a cleaner and a miner. But he had soon learned that rich people liked to become richer, and knowing how to feed their greed had, in turn, made him very rich.

'Where is my daughter?' he asked,

when he entered the main office.

'She's gone out,' said one of the secretaries. 'She went hours ago, before lunch, and she hasn't come back since. I think it was something to do with what's on the television.'

'Oh yes,' said Summers, lazily glancing at the screen. 'And what is on the television?'

'Have you not seen it, sir? We did try to contact you but you must have been out of range.'

'Contact me? About what?'

'The train sir. The Nice to Cariastan train. It's been hijacked.'

'Good God, why didn't you send someone to look for me?' said Summers, storming to his office, which was in the corner of the building.

'We tried but . . . ' The secretary ran after him, and a few others followed her. They knew that the rest of the day was about to get very bad for them, and may even end up with at least one of them being sacked. Quite a few of the original staff had been dispensed with,

with Summers' people put in their place. 'But as I said, sir,' she said breathlessly, when they had reached the office. 'You were out of range and we did send someone to the golf course but they said . . . '

'Yes, yes, never mind that now.' Summers waved his hand, dismissively. 'You'd better bring me up to speed. And someone find out where the hell my daughter has gone.'

After half an hour of chewing up both furniture and employees, Alexander Summers shut the door to his office and went to sit down alone.

They had not told him anything he did not know, but he prided himself on doing a good job of pretending ignorance. As for his anger, he could switch it on and off at will. It still gave him a thrill to see people quivering in his presence. Sometimes he came in to work in a bad mood just to cheer himself up by terrorising everyone.

He took a mobile phone out of his pocket. None of his people would have recognised it or the number, and at the end of the day he would throw it away. But for now it was his only contact with the train. He dialled Karloff's number, but only got a message saying the phone was switched off. If Karloff was sensible he would have dumped his phone as soon as he jumped off the train. If he was still alive. Never mind, Summers would deal with the cowardly terrorist at some other time.

He tried his son's phone, but again got a message saying the phone was unavailable. The same happened with Patty's phone. The train must be in a bad reception area. Damn! He had to know about the child, and whether he was still on the train. Everything depended on the boy being there for the plan to work, one way or another. If the boy died, then all the evidence that Summers had put together blaming Prince Henri for the death of his nephew would be put into place. If the boy survived and Henri stepped down as Summers hoped, then he would put his grandson on the throne and rule as the boy's Lord Protector. Cariastan would be his, and he would ensure that it would remain his even when the boy was old enough to rule in his own right. His backers were relying on him, and he would deliver, as he always had.

His daughter would be a problem. She was far too attached to the boy. But Summers had always been able to bully his children into doing what he wanted with the same temper that terrified his staff.

It made him wonder how Vicky had managed to keep the secret of Solomon's father from him until the man Ambroise turned up and inadvertently gave the news of Prince Philipe's death to Alexander Summers. It made him wonder what other secrets his daughter had kept from him. Never mind. There was plenty of time for that once his plan had come to fruition. It did not occur to him that his anger might encourage those who feared him to keep their secrets even more closely guarded. He was convinced that they were all too frightened to lie to him.

There was a knock on the door of his office. 'Enter!'

'We've found out where your daughter went, sir,' said the same secretary he had reduced to tears earlier.

'Oh yes. Where is she?'

'The concierge on the door said he heard her telling a taxi driver to take her to the Summer Palace.'

That was when Alexander Summers became really angry.

* * *

Faust was called to the palace office, where he picked up the fax he had been waiting for. He read it with a grim expression. It confirmed everything he suspected. But why had the girl not said anything? Was she playing some long game? It did not make sense. It was in her interests to be honest. Unless what she said about not wanting anything was true.

Or maybe it was a double bluff, he thought as he walked to the bedroom where Vicky Summers had been put when she collapsed. She pretended she did not want anything to disarm them until she brought the proof. But why not bring the proof with her in the first place? Why the charade, and why, if she were involved, hijack a train and threaten Cariastan with a nuclear weapon?

Faust shook his head. None of it made sense. He did not want to believe she was innocent, if only because of her relationship with Philipe. Faust had more than one reason for hating Philipe. The playboy prince had once stolen Faust's fiancée from him, promising her a royal marriage. Philipe had dumped her when he grew bored; sending an arrogant message to Faust letting him know the girl was available again.

Had Philipe really changed so much by the time he met Vicky Summers? Could it actually true that the love of a good woman could change a man? If so, then Vicky Summers must be a remarkable young woman indeed. It was something that Faust did not want to contemplate, along with denying the attraction he felt for her despite not trusting her as far as he could throw her.

He found her curled up in a chair in the bedroom, watching the news of the runaway train. 'Is my baby on there?' she asked, looking up at Faust. 'No one will tell me anything.'

'We don't know,' said Faust. 'I'm sorry.' He passed her the fax. 'Were you ever going to tell us?'

Vicky's eyes widened in shock. She jumped up. 'You can't tell. You can't! I'll lose him.' She glanced at the television, her eyes filling with tears. 'If I haven't lost him already. I told you I don't want anything and I meant it. Please, don't tell.'

'I have to. I can't let this remain a secret. If it came out that I knew . . . '

Vicky put her hand on his arm. 'No,

please, Mr. di Luca. I won't ever tell, I promise.'

There was a knock at the door. It was one of the palace staff. 'Excuse me, Miss Summers, but your father is here.'

That was when Vicky Summers looked really frightened. 'You mustn't tell him, not ever,' she whispered to Faust.

'You mean your father.'

'Yes. Please, Mr di Luca, you must help me on this. You don't know what he's capable of. He's used me and my brother all our lives. He used my mother until the pain and humiliation of his cruelty led to her dying of a broken heart. I'd rather my baby was amongst that wreckage than let my father use him too.' It was a shocking thing for her to say, yet she appeared to mean every word of it.

'Very well,' said Faust, warily, as a creeping suspicion began to dawn. 'I won't say anything for now. But we will talk about this later.' He put the fax in his inside jacket pocket.

He could not help noticing how much Vicky trembled as he walked alongside her to the ante room where her father was waiting. Anton was already there, looking pale and worried.

'Oh thank God,' said Alexander Summers, rushing to his daughter and embracing her. 'I came as soon as I heard. I'm so sorry, my darling. I was out of range.' He turned to smile at Anton. 'Perhaps we can talk about improving Cariastan's mobile phone coverage at some point.'

With all the evidence of being a doting father, he turned back to his daughter. 'I hoped that maybe here you would know more about Solomon. Have they found him yet, Your Majesty?' Once again, Summers turned to Anton. He was a man in charge of the situation and did not seem at all fazed to be in the presence of royalty. 'I have unlimited funds, Your Royal Highness. If there is anything I can do to help the hostages on the train, and get my grandson back, just say the word. I am at your disposal, as is my money. Do you think the terrorists will take money? It's worth a try, don't you think? Don't worry, Vicky, darling. We'll get him back for you.'

Faust frowned, the suspicion he had earlier taking full bloom. How to play it, that was the problem. He would have to be careful, because until they knew if the passengers and the little boy were still alive, Faust did not want to do anything to jeopardise their safety.

Vicky pulled away from her father and went to sit down, trembling from head to foot. Faust wanted to go to her, to tell her that everything would be alright. But he did not know if he could even begin to make that promise.

He had a bigger problem. He wanted Summers out of the palace, but how to do so without creating suspicion. Whilst Summers was there, he would see and hear everything they saw. And that might give him an advantage, if Faust's suspicions were correct.

'Actually, Mr. Summers,' he said,

smiling like the good palace aide that he was. 'I think it might be better if you and Miss Summers left Cariastan with the other evacuees.'

'No,' said Vicky. 'I'm staying here until I find out what's happened to Solomon.'

It was exactly what Faust had expected her to say. 'Actually, plans are in place to try to stop the train again at the next border,' he lied. Or at least he hoped it was a lie. Who knew what other countries might do to stop the train passing through their borders? He could see Anton looking at him, quizzically. 'So if you cross over into that country, which you would have to as all planes are grounded in Cariastan, you could be there when that happens.'

'Well, I hope their plan works better than the last one,' said Summers.

'Oh it will. I think they've learned by those mistakes, and apparently they're trying out a new EMP weapons system.'

'EMP?' Vicky looked askance.

'Electro-magnetic pulse,' said Faust. 'It will cut power to the engine — and to everything for a few miles around — but the engine should come to a stop. The hope is that it will disable the bomb too. Then they should have no trouble disarming the remaining terrorists.'

'And they'll all be safe? I mean if they're alive now,' said Vicky.

'Oh yes, perfectly safe. That's the beauty of electro-magnetic pulses. No one can be harmed.'

'Yes,' said Anton, wryly. 'It's a perfect plan. I'm surprised no one has thought of it before.'

'Well, thank God for that then,' said Alexander Summers. He too was frowning, and Faust began to fear he had not been convincing enough. If Summers was as clever as he seemed, he might see through the lie straight away. But he could hardly argue about it, or the plan to remove him and Vicky from the palace without it appearing suspicious.

'We'll arrange transport for you,' said Faust, determined to brook no arguments. 'Anton, a word?'

He and his friend left the room. Further along the corridor, and away from earshot of those in the ante room, Anton turned to Faust and folded his arms.

'Do you mind telling me what that was all about?'

'It's about this being much bigger than a few opportunist terrorists taking a chance on you stepping down for your nephew,' said Faust, grimly.

10

The train hurtled through the countryside. Several times the passengers and hijackers were jostled by a change in tracks. The authorities were clearly trying to reroute the train so that it did not go through too many inhabited areas.

Mike, who had come to about half an hour earlier, could only imagine what arguments were going on behind the scenes, as each country involved understandably wanted nothing to do with a train carrying a nuclear device. Angela had quickly filled him in on what had happened with the little boy, and about Cal's father.

'I think he's the Handler they keep talking about,' she muttered, looking over at Cal, Patty and the remaining gunmen, who stood at the end of the carriage, huddled in a tight group. They appeared to be waiting for instructions. Cal was falling to pieces, Patty remained calm, and the other gunmen looked as if they could go either way.

Mike nodded. 'It makes sense. Only someone with unlimited access to money could pull off a stunt like this. What you say about them replacing King Henri makes sense too. When I was hanging off the side of the train I heard both Patty and Ambroise refer to little Solomon as a prince, and I don't think it was just a term of endearment from Ambroise's point of view.'

'So whoever is behind this hoped to put the child on the throne. The poor little darling. But that doesn't make sense,' said Angela. 'Why put him on the train, in danger?'

'I don't know, but if he had died then I suppose they could make out that the current king in waiting was behind it. You know, getting rid of the competition. If the child could not be king, then the next best thing would be to oust the current king and put a puppet ruler in his place.'

'Maybe King Henri is behind it,' whispered Angela. 'We don't know for certain that Cal's father is behind it.'

Mike shook his head. 'If it looks like a duck and quacks like a duck, then it usually is a duck.'

'Thank you for that bit of wisdom,' said Angela, trying and failing to raise a smile. She looked as tired as Mike felt. They had hardly slept since they left Nice. 'But King Henri could still be behind it all. He could be telling Cal's father what to do. The banker can't take the throne, can he? So how can he gain control over Cariastan? They must have wanted the child out of the way for some reason and the only reason I can think is that he was a threat to the king in waiting. But if that's the case, why not just get rid of him when they had him in their custody? Why go through all this?'

Mike shrugged. 'I don't know. I guess we won't find out until we get off this train.'

'Unless Ambroise . . . Oh Mike, you

don't think I've let that little boy go with a man who intends to kill him, do you?'

Mike took her hand in his. 'It's like you said, if that was their intention they'd have done it whilst they had him. You saw a way for the child to get off the train and you took it. Whatever happens after that is not your fault.'

'He's such a sweet little thing . . . ' Angela's eyes filled with tears. She gazed out of the window, but it was getting dark. The lights from homes far into the distance could be seen, but not much else.

'I never asked you if you had any children,' said Mike, gently.

She shook her head. 'No, I haven't got children. That's the reason I'm on this train, in a roundabout way.'

'What do you mean?'

'I was married once. To Angus Peterson. You know him? He plays a lot of English bad guys in American movies.'

'I've heard of him, yes.'

'We wanted children but I couldn't have them. It was those bloody hot pants, you see.'

'The hot pants?'

'I always had to fit into them. The same pair, every season of *Pandora's Vox*. You don't know what it's like listening to people discussing the size of your bum when you're in the room. I developed an eating disorder because of it. I ended up in a facility to help me deal with it. No one knows, because by then Pandora was old news. It was only later it became cult viewing amongst students. Anyway, it played havoc with my reproductive system. So when Angus and I married, we tried for years to have a baby. But it didn't happen. He wanted to adopt. From Korea or Africa, you know, one of those rainbow coalitions of adopted children that Hollywood stars seem to like collecting.'

'I know what you mean,' said Mike.

'I always felt you should only have children, whether natural or adopted, to love them, not to show off your liberal credentials,' said Angela. 'So we split up because we just couldn't agree on it. Just before I left Britain . . . the reason I left Britain was because I saw Angus and his new wife on the cover of a magazine. She's having his baby. I want to be happy for them. I told the magazine I was happy for them. After all, how could anyone resent a child being born? But inside I was furious and jealous and bitter. I hated myself for feeling that way, but it's not fair. I'd have been a good mum, but now it's too late. I'll never get that chance. Even if we do get off this train.'

'I'm sorry,' said Mike. 'It always amazes me that some people can just churn out children they don't want, whereas others, who would be wonderful parents, just can't make it happen.'

'We tried for years too,' said a voice from the other side of the carriage. It was Liberty Cathcart. 'It does hurt,' she said softly. 'Especially when others around you are able to have children.

It's odd though,' she added, looking at Angela. 'I look at you and think that you have everything I'd like. That lovely face and that wonderful hair. I suppose it goes to show that even if people seem blessed, we shouldn't assume that they are.'

'Thank you,' said Angela, looking surprised at Liberty's sudden kindness.

'It doesn't help,' said Liberty, 'that society judges women by their ability to have children. Even nowadays.'

'No, it doesn't,' said Angela. 'That's what makes me feel such a failure.'

'But you're not,' said Mike. 'You're a great actress.'

'I'm a good actress. Not a great one.'

'*Pandora's Vox* was a marvellous bit of telly,' said Harry Cathcart. 'And not just because of the hot pants.'

'Is it any wonder I'm jealous of you?' said Liberty, smiling at Angela.

'Really? Because I'd love a willowy figure like yours. I spent years trying to get one till I realised I'd need to be six inches taller to pull it off.'

'Oh but I've always wanted curves like yours,' said Liberty.

Mike smiled. Women? Who could ever understand them? They snarled and snapped at each other. Then they found that deep down they were very much the same and suddenly they became best friends.

'I've got a kid and it looks like he's a terrorist,' said Jon Bliss, joining the conversation a bit late.

'Cal's not yours,' said Angela. 'His dad is a banker.'

'Oh.'

Mike noticed that Will was looking at Bliss thoughtfully.

'You er . . . never went with a black woman then?' Will said to the ageing rocker.

'What? Well, yeah there were a few.'

'But you can't remember their names,' Will's voice was tinged with bitterness.

'Well, you know, rock star lifestyle and all that. Women come and go. It's one of the perks.'

'I'd hardly call it a perk, having a kid and not even knowing who he is,' said Will. 'How many more are there out there whose names you don't even know?'

'Hey, lad! Is it Will they call you? What rattled your cage?' asked Bliss. Will fell silent. Angela reached across and squeezed the boy's hand, giving him a smile of encouragement.

Mike thought he knew what was wrong with Will, but did not say anything. Let Will and Bliss work it out between them.

He was more interested in how to wrestle the train back from Cal, Patty and the other gunmen. Cal would be easy enough. He did not seem to have a clue what to do, and appeared to have attended the television school of terrorism, which included strutting about and trying to look menacing. But that probably made him even more dangerous. The other gunmen were disorganised. Patty was a different matter. She was as hard as they came and the others, with no one else to turn to, and not a very good role model in Cal, were taking their cue from her.

'You realise don't you,' Mike said in a loud voice, and looking right at Patty, 'that this train is not going to stop in Cariastan. It's probably going to keep going. If it doesn't hit a building, it will go straight into the Black Sea, and it's going to take you with it. Or they may take the decision to blow the damn thing up before it causes any harm. So how exactly do you plan to get out of this situation? Because jumping off this train is no longer an option. Not at this speed. And neither will you be rescued by helicopter, if that was your original intention. They'll have shut the air space above the tracks down to all but essential flights.'

'Shut up,' said Patty. Mike was gratified to see a glimmer of doubt in her eyes.

'Shut up? That's your answer to the predicament we're all in. You've lost the boy, so you don't have that bargaining power anymore. The rest of the passengers are probably expendable, when compared to the loss of a whole country. The way I see it, the only way we're going to get off this train alive is if we all work together. We need to stop it and quickly, before it crashes. After that, I don't care what happens to you. You can run and get away from the authorities for all I care. But I won't stand by and let everyone on this train be sacrificed to the greater good.'

'He's right, Patty,' said Cal. 'The Handler isn't going to save us now.' There was something approaching heartache in his voice as he said it. 'It was only ever about Solomon and getting him on the throne.'

Patty glared at Cal. 'I am in charge now, because you're obviously too much of a coward. I say what happens on this train and if the vicar doesn't shut up, I'm going to shoot him.'

'How did your father expect to be able to rule Cariastan through Solomon?' asked Angela.

'Who said anything about my father?' said Cal.

'You did, just then. You feel betrayed, and even more so because you're close to the Handler.'

'Don't say a word,' said Patty. 'You'll hang us all.'

'Oh you're finished anyway,' said Mike. 'So you might as well tell us what's been going on here.'

'He's my nephew,' said Cal, glaring at Patty, who was looking at him with a murderous expression in her eyes. 'Solomon is my sister's son. But he's also the son of the late Prince Philipe. He and my sister had a fling, just before he died.'

'So your dad is his grandfather,' said Mike.

Cal nodded. 'And we always do as my dad says, me and my sister Vicky. If Solomon was the king, dad would be the power behind the throne. If Solomon died on the train, then dad was going to blame Prince Henri and destabilise Cariastan that way. There's oil in Cariastan, and dad wants it. Or he wants it for his backers. I don't know who they are.'

'I can guess,' said Mike, thinking of several world powers who might be interested.

'What sort of woman would put a child in that danger?' said Angela, clearly talking about Patty.

'One who's being very well paid and who intends to live to collect her money,' said Patty. She pushed Cal back against the carriage wall, pressing the machine gun under his chin. 'And if you say anymore, I'm going to kill you. Remember that the Handler has already decided you're expendable, so he won't care if you're dead or not.' She pulled him back and shoved him onto the floor, grabbing his gun from him. 'In fact, from this moment on, I'm going to treat you like one of the other hostages.'

'You can't do that,' said Cal. He looked as if he was going to cry. 'Don't forget who the Handler is.'

'He's a man who put his son and grandson on a train that's going to blow up,' said Patty.

Cal slumped against the wall, and dropped his gun.

At that moment, Patty's telephone rang. It was the first communication to the train for some time, so Mike guessed they had been in a bad reception area. 'Yes, sir . . . No, sir, it's all under control . . . The child? Yes, of course the child is on the train. He's sleeping soundly at the moment. Do you want me to wake him? No? Oh, alright then.'

Angela was about to shout and contradict Patty, but Mike put his hand on her arm to stop her. It was better for the Handler to think Solomon was on the train. That way he would not send people looking for the child in Austria. It might also stop the authorities shooting at the train. The rest might be expendable, but a prince of royal blood was not. The Cariastan Royal family were probably related to the British

209

Royal family. Thanks to Queen Victoria, most of the European royals were. Queen Elizabeth II, though only a figurehead monarch, still commanded the respect of most of the world, and those countries would not allow anyone of her blood to die. The fact that Solomon was only a toddler would add to the public condemnation of any act against him. It was awful to think it, and Mike hated using the little one in that way, but the child was the rest of the passengers' only way of surviving.

Angela looked at him and nodded in agreement, as if catching on to his train of thought very quickly. 'Sorry,' she whispered.

Mike suspected that Patty also knew what a powerful bargaining chip Solomon was, hence her not being honest with the Handler about where he was. Without the child as leverage, then the boss would probably sacrifice Patty and the other gunmen. If he believed the boy was still on the train, he would need his own people to ensure the child played a role in the proceedings.

'There is one problem, however, sir,' Patty was saying. 'Cal Summers has thrown his lot in with the hostages. I'm not sure what you want me to do with him . . . Yes, of course. It's your decision, but I will abide by it. Well, these things happen, don't they? He never was strong enough for this, but you can rely on me, sir. Really, sir? That's very generous, thank you.' After listening to a few more instructions, Patty snapped the phone shut. 'For the avoidance of doubt,' she said to the passengers, 'I am in charge now. We carry on to Cariastan, as planned, and I will live to collect my salary, which has just risen considerably.'

With that, she turned to Cal on the floor and pointed the machine gun at him.

'If you kill him, you lose all leverage,' said Mike. 'Because I will certainly let the Handler know that the child is gone next time he rings.'

'Not if I shoot you first, Reverend.'

'You'd have to shoot all of us,' said Angela.

'Excuse me,' said Liberty. 'Why are we sticking up for one of the terrorists?'

'Because he's just a kid,' said Angela.

'He knew enough to put people in danger,' said Liberty.

'So you're happy for her to shoot him?' said Angela.

Oh dear, thought Mike. That must have been the shortest friendship ever. Angela and Liberty looked at each other daggers.

Mike was reminded of the saying about the female of the species being deadlier than the male. Angela and Liberty were both good women, and whilst they might snarl at each other because they were afraid, it did make him fear Patty even more than he had feared Karloff.

'Leave him be, Patty,' Mike said. 'He's just a stupid young boy who's in way over his head. And the more hostages you hold, the more chance you have of getting off this train alive.'

'I'll let him live for now,' said Patty with a smug grin. 'But he can sit with you lot. The king is dead. Long live the queen.'

11

The train thundered on through the early evening, followed overhead by helicopters filming its progress. Some were from the media and others were sent by the various governments, including Cariastan's.

Other helicopters and planes filmed the exodus of people in Cariastan and surrounding countries as they evacuated the area. The roads were jammed, as cars stood nose to tail. The borders were bottlenecks of bureaucracy as each country wanted to get their own people out of harm's way but were less keen on letting others pass through.

'How could you get involved in this?' Will asked Cal. His former friend sat across from him, looking beaten and dejected. If anything Cal was more afraid than the rest of the passengers. They could share their fears with each other, and whilst it did not lessen their terror, it did help that they were all in it together. Cal was neither accepted by the terrorists or the other passengers. Why Will should feel pity for his friend after all he had done, he did not know, but he did.

'You don't know how lucky you were not to have a father,' said Cal, rubbing his tired eyes.

'Really?' Will tried to harden himself against Cal. 'Excuse me for stating the obvious, Cal, but you've had money all your life, and a mother and father, so please don't give me this poor little rich boy rubbish.'

'But it's true, Will,' said Cal. 'My father is a complete tyrant. I spent every day of my life trying to please him and be the son he wants. But I'm not really cut out for all this. Do you know when I was happiest?'

'When?'

'When we were working on the train last summer, just being normal boys who chat up girls and go out to clubs on our days off.'

'If you were happy doing that, why go along with the hijack?'

'I was trapped, that's why. It would have happened with or without me, and I thought that if I got this one thing right, he would love me. Instead, if the vicar over there hadn't stopped her, my father would have let Patty shoot me.'

'Yeah, well maybe Reverend Fairfax should have let her,' said Will. His words held no real malice. It was not in him to be that unkind.

'You don't mean that.'

'If your dad had told you to, would you have shot me?' Will raised his eyebrow.

'I don't know, Will.'

'I do. You'd have done it.'

'Then why are you even talking to me?'

'God knows. Maybe because some-where deep down I want to think we were real friends. I've had no one all my life, and then you came along and for a while you were my best mate. Except it was all a lie.'

'I've told you. It wasn't. I was happy to be your mate.'

'Yeah, till daddy told you to put my life in danger, along with everyone else on this train.'

'If I said I was sorry, you wouldn't believe me,' said Cal, his eyes filling with tears. 'But I am sorry. I'm going to spend the rest of my life in prison because of this. That's if we don't die first.'

Mike spoke up. 'If you help us, Cal, maybe we can make sure you don't spend your whole life in prison. Tell me about the bomb.'

'He's not going to tell you anything,' said Patty. She did not shoot Cal, but she did use the butt of her rifle to hit him across the forehead. It rendered him unconscious.

'You're going to regret that when the train goes up and takes you with it,' said Mike.

'Shut up, Reverend.'

* * *

Liberty and Harry Cathcart huddled together a few seats away from the action. Liberty gasped when Patty hit Cal in the head, hiding her face in her husband's shoulder.

'How did we ever get into this?' she whispered, shivering against him. She wished she was back in Stony End, baking cakes and arranging flowers. They may be boring, but they were nice and safe. Liberty had become used to safety.

'I seem to remember that you wanted to follow the vicar on holiday,' said Harry. 'I told you it was a bad idea.'

'Yes, you did, didn't you?'

'Are you admitting you're in the wrong, dear?'

'I seem to be, don't I?' Liberty smiled sadly. 'Why do you put up with me?'

'I suppose it's because I love you.'

'Thank you for that. You've been so good to me, Harry and I know I'm not always good to you.'

'Yes you are. You take care of me, like you take care of everyone, in your own way.'

'I get on people's nerves.'

'Only because you try too hard, dear.'

She sighed. 'It's because I can't shake the feeling that nothing I do is quite good enough. I know what you took on when you married me. Even Mr. Karloff seemed to know judging by the way he called me madam.'

'I told you then and I'm telling you now that it doesn't matter to me.'

'No, it never did, did it? That's why I love you. Sadly it matters to me. I want to forget that old life, but I can't. So every day I try to be something I'm not, in an attempt to put it behind me. I know everyone in the village laughs at me and that the other villagers find me tiresome. I haven't done very well with Michael's new friend either, and she seems a nice enough sort. I just live in terror of them ever finding out.'

'It wouldn't matter if they did. It

wouldn't change how I feel about you.'

'No, but it will change the way they feel about me. They wouldn't just find me tiresome. I'd be a laughing stock. And so would you. It's occurred to me that if we die on this train, I'll just be remembered as that awful woman from the WI, who acts with all those airs and graces. I don't think I want to be that woman anymore, but now it's far too late to change.'

'Liberty, my love, I don't want you to change. I just want you to be happy with yourself and with me.'

'I've always been happy with you, Harry, even if I haven't always shown it. I'm just afraid I haven't made you happy.'

'But you have. I was all alone and then you came along and I wasn't alone anymore. So what if the villagers find us both tiresome? I know I'm considered an old bore, and I probably am. Everyone has some little quirk and foible about them that others don't much like, and it doesn't make them bad people. But we have something that others don't.'

'What's that?'

'We have each other.'

She smiled up at him and then put her head back on his shoulder. 'At least we'll be together at the end.'

Harry kissed her head. 'It's everything an old bore like me could have hoped for.'

★   ★   ★

'Will?' Jon Bliss called softly across the carriage. All the other passengers, despite the extreme tension, had started to doze. It was as if they had all been told to hurry up and wait. Despite the speed of the train, nothing very much seemed to be happening, and that lulled people into a false sense of security.

'What?' Will said. He was using the First Aid kit to clean up the wound on Cal's head.

'Is it true what Cal said about you growing up without a mum and dad?'

'Yeah, so what of it?'

'So who brought you up? Grandparents?'

'At first they did, but they died when I was little. Then I was in care homes and foster homes. I did well in school though,' he added proudly. 'That's why I'm going to university.'

'Good lad. You should never let anything hold you back.' Jon hesitated. 'I've been thinking, and I remember a black girl from way back. Her name was Marcie.'

'Oh yeah . . . ' Will did not look up, but it was clear he had started to listen more avidly.

'Yes, she was a lovely lass. It wasn't a one night stand. I want you to know that. We spent a nice couple of weeks together, and it might have lasted longer, but then I had to go on tour and the other lads had a strict no girlfriends rule. Mainly so they could get any girl they wanted on tour. We were gone for nearly two years, what with our record taking off and everything. When I came back, I looked for her, but her friends said she had died. I was really sorry to hear it.'

'She had cancer,' said Will. Jon saw a tear roll down the boy's cheek, and he swallowed back a lump that had risen in his throat. 'She only found out while she was carrying me. She refused chemotherapy because it would have harmed me. My grandparents never really recovered from losing her, so I was alone from the age of five. I mean, the care homes and foster parents all did their best. I wasn't badly treated or anything, but it's not the same as having your own mum and dad.'

'I'm sorry. Really I am. I know you think I sound shallow, and I probably do. But I want you to know that your mum wasn't like all the others. She was a nice girl.'

'Thank you for telling me that.'

'What do you say that if we get off this godforsaken train we go out and get a drink and get to know each other?'

'I don't want anything from you. That's not why I sent the letter.'

'Why didn't you just tell me who you were?'

'I don't know.' Will shrugged. 'I suppose I wanted you to recognise me. It's a bit daft of me, I know. I mean, why should you?'

'Well, you've got my eyes for a start,' said Jon. 'I can see that now. So what do you say, lad? Are we going to be friends?'

'Let's just say that I hope we live long enough to try.'

'Yeah, me too. Because I've been watching you since all this started, and I couldn't be prouder that a son of mine grew up to be so kind and so brave. I want you to know that, in case we don't get through this.'

Will whispered 'Thanks,' as a tear rolled down his cheek.

Jon wiped his own eyes. Why did this have to happen now? He wanted to know his lad. He thought of all the time he had wasted having what he thought was a good time. The truth was that most of it was a blur. It was only near to the end that he realised he wanted more out of his life and it might be too late for him to put things right.

He took a deep breath, trying to dredge up a courage he did not feel for his son's sake.

★ ★ ★

Angela could see some of the cars on the roads at the side of the tracks, the horrified drivers watching as the train passed by. If this were a film, she pondered, most people would be blissfully unaware of the threat to them. That's how it always seemed to happen in things like *Mission Impossible*, where no one ever learned about the intrigues that were taking place all around them and no one ever questioned explosions or dead bodies lying in the streets.

In real life, people had a right to know if they were in danger from a nuclear device. She guessed that there would be questions in the United Nations, and that some armies were being mobilised. But it all seemed so far away somehow. She felt as if they were in one of those bottles they put ships in. Only in their case it was a train inside the bottle. They had no way of knowing what was going on in the outside world, apart from what they saw at the side of the tracks. It was a strange thing, heading towards danger, yet they all sat there, doing nothing, as if they were on a day out to the seaside. Only the stricken expressions on all the faces said otherwise.

She wondered if her mum and dad were aware of the danger she was in. They were very elderly and she hated to think of them worrying about her, their youngest daughter. She assumed that they must know. It would be all over the news, and the media would be concentrating on the negative aspects. That was what made a news story. Whilst Meredith and Andrew Cunningham were both in very good health for their age, she still feared that the stress might have an adverse effect on them. Even if she came out of it alive, they might not recover from the worry. And if they lost her . . .

She tried to push the thought aside, but she had never felt so afraid. She wanted to die bravely, but was not sure she was cut out for that when every nerve tingled with fear.

What's more, she had only just found Mike. It was like a huge cosmic joke, giving her everything she had ever wanted, just before snatching it away from her. She remembered all the times she had wasted longing for a child she could not have. She could have just been getting on with her life, instead of concentrating on something that could not be.

The thoughts of children led her to wondering where Ambroise and little Solomon were. She wished she could ask her father to remember them both in his prayers. She had not prayed for a long time. Not properly. She realised that she could ask Mike to pray, but what good would that do? This was a time for positive action, not prayers. Or maybe they could manage a bit of both. What was it they said about God helping those who helped themselves?

'Can they stop the train?' she asked Mike in a low voice. 'Without the bomb going off?'

'I don't know,' he said. 'It's like I said earlier, it depends what sort of bomb it is. That's why it has to be disabled. I would have tried, only it was more important to stop us crashing when I was in the engine cab. I didn't have time to find it, but I know it's in the engine block somewhere.'

'I could try being ill again,' she suggested.

'That's not going to work with her,' he said, nodding towards Patty. 'Besides, whereas Karloff would not shoot you, she might, and I don't want that to happen.'

'Next time I want to run away, I

think I'll just go to the seaside,' she said, remembering hazy days on the beach with her mum and dad.

'Skegness is nice. Nothing ever happens there. We could go there,' said Mike.

'We?'

'Well, if you wanted the company.'

'I'd love the company,' she whispered, her eyes filling with tears. 'It's not fair. You're the perfect man. Brave, handsome, kind. And I'm going to lose you before I even had a chance to find you.'

'I'm not perfect at all, Angela. Far from it.'

'Well, let me pretend that you are for a while.' She put her head on his shoulder. 'Because it makes me feel better.'

Mike kissed the top of her head. 'Okay, we'll pretend for a while that we're both perfect and that if we get out of this we'll fall madly in love and get married.'

'Where will we live?'

'It's up to you. Midchester or Stony End? I don't mind.'

'Yes, I could do with a nice little village where only murders happen. All this nuclear bomb and speeding trains stuff is a bit too exciting for my blood. I'm not sure I'd make a very good vicar's wife though.'

'You'll be a perfect vicar's wife. You're beautiful, kind and brave. Don't think I haven't realised that you could have jumped off the train when Ambroise left with Solomon.'

'Oh but I'd probably have broken a nail or something. I do have my image to think of.'

'Really? And there was I thinking you didn't have a vain bone in your body.'

'You have no idea . . . Besides, I couldn't leave you. You need me.'

'I do?' He then changed it from a question to a statement. 'I do.'

A tear fell down Angela's cheek. 'It's not going to happen, is it? You and me, living happily ever after in Stony End? Even if we get off the train, we've known each other, what? Just over twenty-four hours? People only fall in love that quickly in films. In real life we have to be more sensible. Get to know each other and all that. I'd have to find out you don't put the loo seat down. You have to know that I always leave the top off the toothpaste. We have to be together long enough to forgive each other for those bad habits before rushing into marriage. Not to mention that if we survive this, life will never be this exciting again. Because that's all that's keeping us together at the moment. A shared danger.'

'I'm sorry you've decided to divorce me before we've even had a chance to get married.'

'We'll just have to face the fact that a love like ours was just too perfect to last, Mike. It was nice knowing you and all that.'

Mike laughed but there was sadness behind the sound. 'You really are the maddest woman I've ever met, do you know that? I can't imagine that life with you could ever be boring. So I'm saying that the wedding is back on. Even if I have to drag you down the aisle.'

'I do love it when you're being all masterful.'

'Honestly,' said Patty, coming over to their table, 'if we had any rooms left on the train, I'd send you to one. But as we don't, just shut up, will you? You're giving me a bloody headache.'

'Or you'll do what?' asked Angela. 'Kill us? I think we're all pretty much stuffed here as it is, don't you? And that includes you, regardless of what you think you've been promised. If a man can ask to have his own son shot, I don't think he's going to care about an employee.'

Once again, Patty's eyes flickered uncertainly. 'Cal was going to die because he was weak.' She was about to say something else when there was a cacophony of noise overhead.

Angela and Mike looked out of the window. Helicopters that had been keeping a distance until then were swooping back down towards the train. Only Angela guessed they weren't the same helicopters. It was hard to tell in the dark, but they looked bigger. More like . . .

'Gunships,' Mike said, urgently. 'It's an air strike! Get down everyone!' He pulled Angela from the seat to the ground, and everyone else followed suit.

Their lives and the train became an appalling battlefield, as the guns on the choppers shot out the windows, shattering the glass and crockery inside the restaurant car. Bottles of spirits exploded and filled the air with the aroma of alcohol. This was mixed with the smell of cordite from the bullets. Some of the gunmen were hit, as they tried to fire back. Angela saw Patty slump into a corner, and realised she had been hit. Despite Patty's behaviour, it was sickening to see the impact of the bullets pummelling the woman's body.

Some of the passengers were also hit, crying out as the lights in the carriage were hit, descending everyone into darkness.

'I can't believe they did it,' Angela sobbed to Mike, the terror she had tried to hide rising to the surface. 'I can't believe they'd rather kill us than find a way to stop the train.'

The air strike probably only lasted a few minutes, but it seemed to go on for hours. Angela clung to Mike, and started to pray. Whether for life or a quick and painless death, she did not know.

★ ★ ★

Faust and Anton watched the news in horror. 'Who is doing this?' asked Anton. 'Is it the government of that country?'

'No,' said the Secretary of Defence, who had been speaking on the telephone. 'They swear they know nothing about this. They're sending in their own people to put a stop to it. No one wants the bomb to explode in their country and that's what might happen because of this air strike. This . . . ' He pointed at the screen in horror and disbelief. 'This is madness.'

More images filled the screen, of planes and choppers going in and engaging those firing at the train. The train looked a wreck, yet kept on its path, speeding along the tracks. Some of those trying to escape in cars on the roadside were caught in the crossfire, leading to carnage on the roads. Anton pondered briefly on the irony of those who had left home seeking safety being harmed in a dogfight.

'Where is Mr. Summers?' asked Anton, turning to one of the palace aides, who was acting as a runner.

'He's still in the palace. He said he cannot persuade his daughter to leave.'

'Good,' said Anton. 'Don't let him leave. Don't let either of them leave. Make up some story about it not being safe out there. Actually, you won't even have to lie. I want Mr. Summers and Vicky brought here to this room, this minute.' He turned to one of the tech people. 'Do you have those reports I asked for yet?'

'No, Your Majesty,' said one of the men.

'So what is taking so much time?' Anton snapped.

'We sent them for analysis, but with having to oversee the evacuation . . . '

'I want them now!'

Faust put his hand on Anton's shoulder. 'They're pushed to the limit as it is, Anton.'

'Yes, of course. I'm sorry,' Anton said to the tech guy. 'I didn't mean to snap at you. Just try and hurry them up for me, please.'

'We'll get him,' Faust whispered, as he and Anton went back to the screen. 'One way or another, he won't leave this palace a free man.'

* * *

'We need to help people,' said Mike, as it seemed World War Three was taking place above them. He crouched along the floor, narrowly missing being hit by a bullet. The lamps had gone out in the carriage, most of them shot out, leaving only ambient lighting by which they could see their way.

'Mike, we have to wait,' said Angela, grabbing his arm. 'You're going to get shot.'

Mike ignored her. He knew what she said was sensible, but people would die if they did not get medical help soon. 'Will, are you hurt?'

'No, sir.'

'I think we can dispense with the 'sir' now, Will. Call me Mike. Is there a first aid kit behind the bar?'

'Yes, sir . . . Mike, but it's only a small one. You know, for if a customer cuts their hand on a glass or something. Or a minor head wound,' he added, pointing to Cal, who he had dragged to the floor during the air strike. 'It's not suitable for gunshot wounds.'

'Never mind, it will have to do. Can you get to it? You're nearer than me.'

As Will crawled to the bar at the end of the restaurant, Patty grabbed him. 'Help me,' she cried.

'Leave her,' said Mike, savagely. 'She can wait till everyone else has been seen to.'

'I've still got a gun,' Patty snapped, waving it weakly above her head.

Will took it from her as easily as taking sweets from a child.

'Not anymore,' he said. One of the gunmen made an attempt to stop him, but he must have realised the game was up. He threw his own gun on the floor, away from Patty. The others who weren't badly injured followed suit. That was something, thought Mike. His life might get a bit easier, if the idiots firing above them stopped and went away.

Will only just managed to get behind the bar. Mike could hear the sound of crunching glass as Will moved around. 'I can't see properly,' Will said.

'Just take your time, lad,' Mike said, kindly.

'I've just thought,' said Will. 'There'll probably be one in the engine carriage too. It's the rules. One first aid kit in each carriage. Though the big one, with the gurney and the defibrillator and what have you was in one of the back carriages.'

'Never mind, we'll make do with what we've got.' Mike looked up, realising that for the first time in several minutes he had not had to shout. The shooting was getting further away.

'Is it stopping?' asked Angela, getting up off the ground.

'It's either stopping or the battle is taking place back there somewhere,' said Mike. 'Let's hope the good guys win.'

People started to move. Those who were injured were laid across two seats, apart from Patty, who was left on the floor near to the end of the carriage. At Mike's behest, the passengers at that end collected up what was left of the machine guns, and brought them to him.

To shouts of protestation, he threw them all out of the window.

'I'm going to die here and no one cares,' said Patty.

'Yep, well that was always a certainty,' said Angela, casting a disgusted glance at her whilst she tended another passenger's wounds. Luckily that was only a flesh wound. 'You were quite willing to kill us all and blow up Cariastan or whatever other country we happened to be travelling through, so tell us exactly why you should have special treatment.'

'His own son and grandson,' Patty murmured, her voice getting weaker. 'He was willing to kill them both . . . '

'She is badly hurt,' Angela said to Mike. He nodded, and Angela went to Patty.

One look at Patty's injured stomach told Angela all she needed to know. Unless they got to a hospital within the next few minutes — and that was highly unlikely — Patty was finished.

'Will I live?' Patty asked.

Angela shook her head, not in the mood to be kind. 'No, you won't. So since you're going to die, perhaps you can tell Mike how to defuse this bomb.'

'I don't know,' said Patty, smiling wanly. 'It wasn't my area. I was just the childminder.' She sounded as if she believed such a job was beneath her. 'They were going to stop the train with an EMP at the next border.' She seemed to be talking to herself. 'I suppose that's why they decided to blow it up instead.'

'Who built the bomb?' asked Mike, going over to where Angela was tending Patty. If they could find that out, then the authorities might be able to arrest the man and he would have to tell them how to defuse it.

'I don't know that either. We were only told what we needed to know.'

'Well do you know exactly where it is?'

'Yes, I can tell you that. It's under a panel on the floor of the engine room. What a mess . . . ' Patty said. It was not clear if she was talking about the train, the bomb or the state of her stomach. They would never know because in that moment she died.

'Will, can you do something else for me?' asked Mike.

'Yeah, anything, Mike, just say the word.'

'Get your . . . I don't know what you'd call him . . . the fat controller or whatever, on the phone and find out if there's a way to stop this train that won't involve blowing it up. I'm going to look for the bomb.'

'I'll come with you,' said Angela.

'No, you won't,' Mike protested. 'You'll stay here. There's not enough space in the engine room anyway.'

'It had two drivers in there before. You told me they both jumped out. Remember?'

'Angela, will you please stop arguing with me when I'm trying to keep you safe?'

'See, this is why we can never marry. One hint of danger and you go all alpha male on me. I'll have you know I've fought dinosaurs. Admittedly they were stop-go animation, but still. Dinosaurs.'

'Well, if I meet any dinosaurs on the way there, I'll be sure to let you know.'

'Come on, Angela,' said Liberty, surprising everyone by getting the name right. 'Let's let the men be men, whilst we women do the hard work of patching up in here. We could do with getting rid of some of this glass.'

Angela clearly did not like being left behind, but she nodded. 'I'd best stay here and do housework with Liberty. I suppose I would be in the way rather whilst you're off saving the universe.'

'I'm not interested in saving the universe,' said Mike. 'Only our little corner of it. We'll be able to make that trip to Skegness then.' He turned and left the carriage, heading for the engine room. Meanwhile Will started making phone calls.

★   ★   ★

243

'Mr. Summers, sir?' The aide came to the room where Alexander Summers was waiting for his daughter. Her absence had given him time to make the necessary phone calls. 'His Royal Highness has requested your presence in the operations room.'

'In that case, we'll come immediately,' said Alexander. 'My daughter is in the bathroom next door. I'll tell her to hurry up.'

Vicky joined them, looking paler than ever when they entered the operations room.

'Ah, there you are,' said Anton, kindly. 'I'm afraid I have some worrying news for you. There has been an air strike, hitting the train.'

Vicky blanched. 'Ordered by you?'

'No, certainly not. We think it was an attempt to cover up the evidence,' said Anton. 'Thankfully the government stepped in and put a stop to it. The train is now heading for the next border.'

'Where the EMP will stop it, I

suppose,' said Alexander Summers.

'Oh that,' said Faust, cutting in. 'Unfortunately that is no longer an option. Military budgets and all that. No, the train is definitely headed for Cariastan. We felt you might like to sit here and watch it with us. Or you could leave with all the evacuees.'

'We'll stay,' said Vicky, firmly. 'Do we know if anyone on the train was hurt during the air strike? Is there any news of Solomon?'

'No, I'm afraid not,' said Anton. 'Please sit down, and I'll have someone bring you some more tea.'

'I'm sick of tea,' said Vicky, becoming emotional. 'I've done nothing but drink tea for half the day. The other half I spend in the bathroom, getting rid of the tea. I just want to know what's happened to my little boy.'

'Now, Vicky,' said her father. 'Please try to keep calm. I'm sure His Majesty and these good people have enough to worry about without your histrionics. Actually, Your Majesty,' he said, looking at his watch. 'My daughter and I will leave after all. I can get her safely out of the country.'

'I'm sorry, that will not be possible now,' said Anton. 'You see, we've stopped anyone coming or going from the palace. Even my good friend Faust insisted on staying behind, despite my protestations. Your window for escaping Cariastan has gone. So all we can do now is sit and hope that someone can stop the train and the bomb in time.'

'This is outrageous,' said Summers. 'We are British citizens. I am sure if you contact our embassy . . . '

'The British Embassy has already been evacuated,' said Faust. 'We apologise for this, but we did give you the option of leaving earlier and you insisted you wished to stay for the sake of your grandson.'

'I do want to stay,' said Vicky. 'If my boy is on that train, then I want to be here when it gets to Cariastan, regardless of what happens.'

'Oh shut up, Victoria,' snapped

Summers. 'If you want to die in this God-forsaken country that is up to you, but I'm not going to. I will leave.' Summers headed for the door but found his way barred by two armed guards. He reached into his pocket for his phone, but a warning look from the guard made him drop it back into his pocket.

'You realise, of course,' said Anton, smoothly, 'that we cannot allow calls in or out of the palace at such a delicate time. Our people are already backlogged going through the calls that have been made from here today, in the hopes of finding out if we have a mole in our midst.'

'What makes you think that?' asked Summers.

'We've had a communication from someone inside the train,' said Faust. 'Our people are working with them to stop the train and defuse the bomb.'

'So you know if Solomon is still alive?' asked Vicky.

'No, I'm sorry, we don't know who is

alive or who is dead. All we know is that someone told the terrorists about the EMP that the other country was planning to use and a few minutes later, the air strike happened.'

'Please,' said Vicky, 'If you speak to them again, ask about my son.'

Faust nodded and exchanged glances with Anton. The girl, at least, was consistent. She only cared about her little boy. For his part, Summers had neither asked about his grandson or his son.

'We do have some bad news,' said Anton, watching for a reaction from both father and daughter. 'It seems your son died during the air strike.' It was not strictly true, but that did not matter. It was Summers' reaction that Anton was waiting for.

'Oh . . . ' Vicky put her hands to her face. 'Oh, poor Cal. Did the terrorists kill him?'

'We don't know that yet,' said Faust. It was a lie. They knew everything now, thanks to the young man called Will who had contacted emergency services. They even knew that Solomon was no longer on the train, but they wanted to keep that information to themselves until they knew exactly what they were dealing with. 'I'm very sorry for your loss, Mr. Summers.'

'Oh God,' said Vicky, immediately putting her hand to her mouth in horror. 'Poor Cal.'

Alexander Summers seemed to have to think about it for a moment, before his shoulders slumped. 'Oh, my dear, darling son,' he said, wiping dry eyes. 'I hope he died bravely.'

'I'm not sure he had the chance for that,' said Anton, his voice tinged with irony. 'So if you will take a seat, sir, Miss Summers, we can get on with trying to stop the train.'

'Can you stop it?' asked Vicky.

'We're bringing in someone to guide the young man, Will, so hopefully we will stop the train,' said Anton. 'And there's Reverend Fairfax, the passenger who was in the Bomb Squad. He's going to see if he can defuse the bomb. We're going to bring an expert in for that too, to help him in any way we can. The next few hours will be crucial.'

'Couldn't we at least watch from a safe distance?' said Summers. 'There's no real need for an act of suicide on our parts, is there?'

Faust answered by pulling a chair out to the middle of the room and gesturing Summers to sit in it. 'What makes you so sure it's going to be an act of suicide, Mr Summers?'

12

Mike prised open the panel on the floor of the engine. It was dark, but he had managed to find a flashlight hanging from a nail in the cab. There was a bottle of whisky too, so he took an edifying swig of that. He did not want to be drunk, but he could use a little more courage. It had been a long time since he had defused a bomb, and he was not sure he still had the skills to do so.

It was hardly like riding a bicycle, because time and bomb technology had moved on. By the time he left the army, they were using remote control robots to disarm bombs. The bomb disposal experts were well away from the scene. Still, he had trained to defuse them at close quarters, because not all bombs were in places where the robots could reach. That still did not mean he could do the same to this device.

'I've got someone on the phone,' said Will, coming into the cab. The lad stopped when he saw the bomb beneath the panel. Even though it was dark, the timer display shone brightly. It was set to go off at midnight, as the train was supposed to be reaching Cariastan. 'Won't we get to Cariastan before midnight?' he asked. 'We're already ahead of time.'

There had been no incidents on their very short trip through the next country. They were supposed to go back through the previous country briefly, but the rails had been redirected, to make sure they carried straight on to Cariastan. They would have another short trip through the southern part of the Ukraine before reaching the border. Then it was only a few short miles to the Cariastan capital.

'Maybe,' said Mike. 'I don't think we can worry too much about the schedule anymore. We just have to stop the damn thing. It's a dirty bomb, just as I thought.'

'What does that mean?' asked Will.

'It means that it's an ordinary bomb, but packed with radioactive material.'

'Oh heck . . . ' Will rubbed his eyes with his hands. For a moment, Mike thought he was going to lose the lad altogether, but Will had the resilience of youth on his side. He recovered relatively quickly. 'Anyway, what was I saying?' he added. 'Oh yeah, there's a man on the phone who's going to help me stop the train. I hope. But I need you out of the way. He says we can't really defuse the bomb and stop the train at the same time because of the size of the cab.'

'I understand,' said Mike. 'I'll stay on the sidelines, but help you if and when I can.'

'Thanks. I'm not sure I'll be very good at this.' Will put the phone onto the dashboard and hit the speaker button. 'This is Will speaking,' he said. 'I'm in the cab now and Reverend Fairfax is with me.'

'Very well,' said a voice at the other

end. 'Tell me what you see? Is the brake lever in one piece?'

'I'm afraid not,' said Mike, cutting in. 'I broke it when I was trying to stop the train before. Hence us not being able to stop now.'

'It is possible you broke the cable by pulling the lever too hard,' said the man at the other end.

'Do you have a name?' asked Will. 'It will be easier than just thinking of you as a voice.'

'I am sorry. Yes, call me Gregor, please.'

'Thanks, Gregor,' said Will. 'I'm Will and my friend here is Mike. So if the brake cable is broken, what can we do to mend it?'

'I am not sure if you can. It depends if you have spares on board. If so, they will be in a compartment in the engine block. But even then, you need to reconnect the cable to the brake mechanism. That involves climbing through the gap in the cab and reaching the wheels from there. And all while the

254

train is moving at that tremendous speed.'

'We might have a bit of a problem with that,' said Mike. 'The gap leading to that mechanism is where the bomb is. I don't fancy crawling around it and I'm definitely not going to ask Will to do it. It could set it off just by contact. Surely there's some other way. What if they rerouted us onto a different track? Won't that help to slow us down?'

'If you do not want to crash first,' said Gregor. 'So far the changes in track have been smooth and in a virtual straight line, but for it to stop the train, the change would have to be on a severe curve. That could throw the train off the tracks and cause the very accident that you are trying to prevent.'

'What if we disengaged the carriage from the engine?' asked Mike. 'It would stop the carriage, right?'

'Eventually,' said Gregor. 'Yes, but the engine . . . '

'Never mind the engine,' said Mike. 'We'll worry about that if and when we defuse the bomb. Then you can arrange something at the other end to stop the engine. It won't matter if it crashes once the bomb has been defused.'

'What are you suggesting?' asked Will.

'Come back to the carriage and I'll explain it,' said Mike, switching Gregor off for a moment.

Mike assembled all the remaining passengers and gunmen together. 'There is no way to stop the engine. Not at the moment,' he explained. 'But we can detach this carriage from the engine. I can't promise where you'll end up. Hopefully it will be a place of safety. But you'll be alive. I gather that Cariastan has been mostly evacuated. What I suggest is that when this carriage stops, you all start running in the other direction and keep going, until you find a road and a way to get out of the path of the bomb should it go off.'

'That's a great idea,' said Angela. 'When do we do it?'

'As soon as possible,' said Mike. 'Will

can help me detach the engine.'

'No,' said Angela. 'Please, let me help you to do this. Will, I'm not suggesting you can't do it, sweetheart. You're a really brave and resourceful young man. In fact if I were twenty years younger I'd marry you. But as the remaining healthy staff member on this train, I think you should stay with the rest of the passengers and crew and steer them to safety.'

'Yeah, alright,' said Will, looking doubtful.

'She's right,' said Jon Bliss. 'We need you here, Will. Actually, I'm being selfish. I need you here. I'm not saying goodbye to you again that quickly.'

The lad looked proud then. 'Okay . . . Dad.'

'I'm not going to talk you out of this, am I?' Mike said to Angela.

'Not a chance.'

'Okay. If you insist on helping, you can help. But we're both coming back to the carriage anyway.'

'I think that's probably the first time

you've lied to me,' she said. 'Well not the first time. There was the whole omitting to tell me you were a vicar thing, but I mean a real out and out lie. Because I know there's no way you're going to let that bomb go on its merry way to Cariastan, Mike Fairfax.'

'Let's just get the carriage detached and then we'll argue about it,' said Mike.

A few minutes later, taking a computer tablet with the schematics that Will had downloaded for him, he led her to the gap between the carriage and the engine. It was covered with a piece of thick concertina rubber. 'Hold the torch for me,' he said, pulling up the flooring to reveal the joint and the tracks below them. He looked at the schematics, and at how the two carriages were joined together. He had to release the pneumatic valve that bound them together, and undo the pins on two snatch plates that stopped them from coming apart, along with several other pins. It was a tricky business, and the movement of the track beneath the train made both Mike and Angela feel queasy as they worked.

He had moved to the other side of the gap, nearest to the engine. When Angela went to follow him, he said, 'No, I need you that side. There's no room here for us to kneel side by side. Besides, you can reach the final snatch plate easier than I can from there.'

'Mike?' Angela asked, as they worked.

'Hmm?'

'I've told you what I was running away from. What were you running away from? Liberty said something about a breakdown.'

'Oh that. Well . . . ' For a moment, he was not going to tell her, but then he realised it would do him good to unload, especially when they were so near to the end. He might never get the chance to be honest with Angela again, and he owed her honesty when he knew he was planning to deceive her again. 'It was something that happened in Stony End last year. A little girl went missing.'

'I think I heard about that on the news.'

'Yes, it was a big case. Her parents weren't deeply religious. In fact I think they only came to church for her nativity play one year. They always do it at the church instead of the school. It's nice. One of my favourite times of year. Because Christmas is all about children, isn't it?' He realised that he was prevaricating, because he could not bring himself to get to the crux of the matter. 'Anyway, they turned to me for spiritual help when she went missing, and of course I gave it to them. It's a sin to say it, but I felt proud to be needed in their hour of darkness. The whole village helped them, not just me. The villagers were up all night, for several days, taking it in shifts, to find her. I went to the family home every day, and just listened to them as they talked about her. I wanted so much to help them, to bring their little girl back for them, and I felt helpless. I even stopped the police from bothering them

260

too much, because the emotional toll of being questioned was so high, especially for the mother. So the police, because they respected me, went away and explored other avenues.' He stopped speaking for a moment. This was partly to concentrate on disengaging the carriage and partly because the next bit of his story was still too painful to recount. 'They found her in the end. The little girl I mean. She had been right under me all along when I visited the house. They had kept her in the cellar. I had been the one to stop the police from continuing the search in the house and finding her . . .'

'Oh Mike, I remember now,' said Angela, nodding sadly. 'Her parents had done it thinking they would make a fortune from the papers.

'In my next sermon, I railed against the parents and a God that would let such a thing happen, but most of all against myself for being so blinded to the truth. For letting her evil parents flatter me with their confidences to the point that I actively stopped a perfectly reasonable part of the police investigation. I felt such a bloody fool. That was my breakdown,' he said, as the horrific memory filled his head. 'I dared to speak the truth about how I felt about the whole awful event. Oh they were very nice to me, everyone, even the bishop. But I'm a marked man now, as far as the Church is concerned. I won't ever rise any higher . . . not that I care about that . . . and I'm sure the next time a family need spiritual help in Stony End, they won't turn to me for fear of me turning on them.'

'But the parents deserved it, Mike. Everything you said, they deserved it. I bet more people cheered you than condemned you.'

'It isn't the way a vicar should behave. I'm supposed to forgive people. That's what the New Testament is all about. But I could not forgive that man and woman for using their child in such a way.'

'And you couldn't forgive yourself for

letting them fool you,' Angela said gently.

'No. I keep thinking that if I'd let the police do their job, the child might have been found sooner.'

'What happened then is not a good reason to sacrifice yourself to this now, Mike.'

'I'm not sacrificing myself.'

'I think that you are. You're making sure everyone is safe and then you're going to try to defuse the bomb. If you fail . . . '

'Could you try to have a bit more faith in me?'

'I do have faith in you, Mike. I've only known you for a day or so, and yet I'm putting my life in your hands. All the other passengers are doing the same. That's the trust you engender in people. And if an evil man and woman took advantage of your innate goodness, it's not your fault. You were in an impossible situation. No one wants to believe that parents would do such a thing to their child. I won't stand by and let you punish yourself for it.'

He smiled softly at her. Why did she have to come into his life now when there might not be anything he could do about it? It was almost as if God was taunting him with the happiness he could know, if he survived long enough to enjoy it.

'I'm not punishing myself. No one else on the train can defuse this bomb, so I've obviously been sent here for a reason. I couldn't save the child from her vile parents, but I will save the people on this train, and any others who may be harmed by this bomb. I'm just trying to do the right thing, Angela.'

'I know you are. That's why I can't bear to let you go. It's like I said. You're the perfect man. It's just not fair that we've only just met when it might be too late.'

'I feel the same way, so we'll make a deal. When all this is over, we'll find a nice restaurant in Cariastan and get to know each other properly.'

'That's a date, Reverend Fairfax. So you'd better not stand me up.'

'I'll be there. You just make sure you are.'

'We'll both be there. Because we're doing this together. I'll be with you every step of the way.'

Mike nodded. He went back to concentrating on separating the carriages. There was one pin left, and it seemed that Angela had not noticed where he had deliberately put her. That was good. She would be angry with him, but she would be alive, and that was all that mattered.

'This is it,' he said, 'one more pin and the carriage will be separated. It will carry on for a while, but without the engine to pull it, it should come to a natural stop.'

'Okay,' said Angela.

He paused momentarily, thinking of Jamie. When the day was over, his son might be without both parents. Would Jamie understand why Mike had left him? Or would he be angry about

265

his father's sacrifice. It was not only Jamie Mike thought of in those final moments.

He took one last look at Angela before he took the pin out, taking in her beauty, and her Titian curls. If he had to choose one last thing to see before he died, he could not have chosen better than Angela's lovely face. A thousand regrets ran through his mind. That he had not met her sooner. That he had not kissed her more. That he had not told her that, despite their banter, none of the things he said to her were a joke.

'I'll see you at the restaurant,' he lied, and then he pulled the final pin out.

The carriage jerked a little, keeping pace with the engine to begin with, because of the momentum. Then it started to separate. One foot . . . Two feet . . . Three feet . . .

'Mike!' Angela called, as the gap widened. She stood up and by the light of the moon he could see her eyes flashing with fury at his deception.

'What?'

'Did I tell you I used to do all my own stunts?'

She took a step back and then leapt across the gap, her arms and legs flailing in the dark, as the gap grew wider still.

With growing horror, Mike realised that she was going to fall onto the tracks and be crushed by the restaurant car.

13

Angela clung on to Mike for dear life as the train tracks rattled beneath her and her legs flapped just above them. He had just managed to catch her hand, almost dislocating her shoulder in the process. But she was still alive.

The carriage bearing the rest of the passengers had fallen way behind. Will had come to the connecting door, and was watching them as they sped away. He waved, and put a thumb up, wishing them luck.

'You idiot!' Mike cried, dragging her back into the relative safety of the engine cab. She did not have time to wave back to Will. Angela's legs, though on solid ground, were shaking uncontrollably. 'Why on Earth did you do that?'

'I did it because you don't have to be alone.' She did not care if he was angry with her. There was no way he could make her stay with the others now.

'Angela, what you just did is suicidal. It's not just that you could have been crushed by the carriage. This engine could blow up and take everything with it. How could you be so stupid?'

'And what you're planning to do isn't suicidal? Be honest, Mike. You were never going to sacrifice the passengers. This was what you were going to do all along.'

'Maybe. I don't know. But there's no reason for you to be at risk. Now I have to look after you too.'

'No, Mike,' Angela said, taking him firmly by the shoulders. Her voice trembled with emotion. Partly because of the jump she had just made and partly because she was so angry with him. 'You don't have to look after me. I've managed quite well for forty-five years to look after myself. I'm here to look after you, because if I don't, no one else will. At least not here, when you need it most. I can't do much, but I can cheer you on.'

'You're quite mad,' he said, sounding a little less angry.

'Actresses usually are.'

'Hmm,' he murmured.

Angela knew that she had probably blown it with him, as far as having a relationship was concerned. What she had done was stupid. She could have been nice and safe with the other passengers. But something had drawn her to Mike from the very beginning, and that same something was telling her that she needed to be with him now. Maybe it was a higher power, or maybe it was her own vanity, but either way, she was going to listen to the voice that told her to stay by him. 'If you want to play the macho hero, fine,' she told him. 'But even a macho hero needs his hand held sometimes.'

If he told her to get lost afterwards — assuming there was an afterwards — then so be it. She was surprised to find that the idea made her heart ache. But she had made her choice and she would not back down now. 'So what do you need to do now, soldier?' she asked, trying to sound business-like. 'How do you defuse this bomb? Cut the red wire? Blue wire?'

'Oh don't confuse me before I've even started. I need to take a closer look at it.' Mike knelt down and pulled the panel from the floor of the engine. Once again they could see the tracks speeding beneath them. He fiddled with a torch, and it almost fell down the hole.

Angela caught it. 'See,' she said, holding it aloft for him. 'You do need me. For this anyway.'

He glanced at her but did not answer. He had become someone else. Someone she did not recognise. Angela guessed that the men in his bomb disposal squad would recognise him though. His eyes took on an intense look as he checked every part of the bomb. The timer said they had an hour left, but they were less than an hour away from Cariastan. The train would get there before midnight. The border was only a few miles away.

'I know how this works,' she said. 'The timer will go right down to one and then it will stop and we'll be saved. Sorry,' she added, when she saw the irritation in his eyes. 'I'll shut up and just hold the torch like a good girl.' She silently cursed the nerves that always made her talk too much. If she was not careful, he might decide to fling her from the cab and out into the darkness. She shuddered at the thought, even though common sense and her knowledge of Mike so far told her that he would do no such thing.

'We might well go right up to the hour,' he said eventually, after he had finished examining the bomb.

'What do you mean?'

'The bomb is booby trapped. This is something we always had to beware of when defusing a bomb. Sometimes the bomb maker would make it seem that you could defuse it just by clipping a particular wire, but that wire would actually detonate the whole thing early.'

'And this is what they've done?'

Mike nodded. 'Yes. But I know this bomb.'

'Know it? How? Does it have a name? Were you once friends?'

Mike sighed. 'I know the bomb maker's work. I've seen it before, when I was in the army.'

'That always happens too,' said Angela. 'In films, I mean. It'll be some bloke you put in prison.'

'We're just one big walking cliché, aren't we?' Mike said, raising a wry eyebrow.

'Yes, I suppose we are.' Somehow Angela did not think they were talking about the bomb anymore. But she would not go there. She would prove to him that she was not the useless little woman.

It was odd but she had always assumed that if someone knew they were going to die, the time went quickly. Instead it felt as if her life were in slow motion, making the fear last longer. She had hoped that once she had made a decision to stay with Mike no matter what, the fear would go. But it was still there, and seemed to strike more deeply with each passing second.

'So what do we do next?' asked Angela, just to break the agonizing silence.

'I must try to remember how the bomb was booby trapped before.'

'What do you remember? Come on, tell me. It might help.'

'I remember that we thought it should be the red wire.'

'But it was the blue wire?'

'It wasn't as simple as that. Both red and blue wires were hooked up to the detonator and any disturbance to either would have set the bomb off. There was another wire hidden inside the . . . ' Mike started. 'That was it. There was a third wire. If I can find that, I may be able to cut it and stop the whole thing. If not, we'll go to Plan B. Sorry you came with me now?'

'No, not at all. I said you shouldn't

be alone and I stand by it.' So why did she want to jump off the train? She steeled herself against the impulse. She would not abandon Mike now, no matter how terrified she was.

Reaching over the gap in the floor, Mike took Angela by the shoulders and kissed her on the lips. If he meant to console her it did not work. It only reminded her of what she would miss by dying that night.

'Will Plan B work?' she asked, gulping back tears. 'If you don't defuse the bomb?'

Mike nodded. 'Hopefully. Usually the biggest threat from a dirty bomb comes from the actual explosion, but in a small city like the capital of Cariastan that explosion would be pretty bad. The radiation leak afterwards is not as high as people imagine it will be. It's the psychological trauma that's worse, as people can't see or feel radiation, so they don't know if they're going to ingest it. Yes, some will die from the radiation, but no one knows who, and that's the real power of a dirty bomb. Some call it a weapon of mass disruption rather than a weapon of mass destruction.'

'Poor us . . . '

'Yes,' said Mike. 'Poor us. I can't even swim,' he added.

Angela did not quite understand why he was bringing that up now. 'It was rather a blow to my hero worship of you, but I'll get over it.'

'Well, you've got a whole ten minutes to come to terms with it.' Mike fiddled with the bomb. Angela could see beads of sweat on his brow. When a droplet fell into her eye, she realised he was not the only one sweating. 'Wish us luck.'

'Good luck us,' said Angela. She held her breath, waiting for the explosion that followed.

Mike snipped at the wire. Nothing happened. The timer kept on with its countdown, with about fifteen minutes left. 'Well, swimming it is,' he said. 'You ready?'

'No, not really.'

'I'm sorry.'

'There's no need to be, Mike. You did your best.'

'No, I mean I'm sorry I wasted time being angry with you for coming with me and I'm sorry we won't get to go out for that dinner in Cariastan, or go home to Stony End and get married.' Mike slammed the cover shut on the cab floor, hiding the bomb and the countdown from them. Angela listened in horror as he phoned through his plans to the relevant authorities.

'Maybe we will meet in some other life,' said Angela when he had finished. Standing up, she took hold of his hand and put her head on his shoulder, turning her face against it to hide from what was to come. The train sped through the capital city and out of it again, into the suburbs of Cariastan. Then it went past those suburbs and into the docklands area on the edge of the city. The train kept going, along more tracks, and right up to a jetty, which was used for loading and unloading directly from ships and onto the freight trains. At the end of the jetty was a pair of buffers, but they were no match for a speeding engine.

Mike and Angela clung to each other as it crashed through the buffers and then ran out of tracks and hurtled into the water, sending a plume of water up into the night sky.

14

The carriage holding the other passengers came to a stop somewhere in the Ukraine. Everyone on board breathed a sigh of relief. Within minutes, a rescue crew had arrived, bringing ambulances and a minibus with which to ferry the passengers to a place of safety.

But first the police boarded the train, and rounded up all the gunmen, as pointed out to them by the passengers.

Will watched sadly as Cal was taken away in handcuffs. 'I'll come and visit you in jail,' he said.

'Why would you bother?' asked Cal.

'Because I think you need a friend,' said Will. He turned to the father he had just found and they left the train together.

'Why don't you come on tour with me?' Jon suggested. 'I'm off to America next month, and I could do with another roadie.'

'Yeah, why not?' said Will. 'I can't imagine there'll be a Midnight Train for a while. I have to be back for September and university though.'

'Oh don't worry,' said Jon. 'You will be. I intend to make sure you get your education lad.'

'Typical,' said Will, with a grin. 'I get a father for five minutes and already he's bossing me around.'

'Not bossing you around. Just making sure you do what your mother would have wanted.'

'Yeah, you're right. She would.'

Jon put his arm around his son's shoulder and they walked towards the mini bus.

Liberty and Harry Cathcart were not too far behind them. 'I feel as if I want to kiss the ground,' said Liberty.

'Don't let me stop you, dear,' said Harry.

'Oh really, Harry, as if I would. The floor might be filthy.'

'That's my girl,' said Harry, giving her a kiss. 'Back to normal. I was worried for a minute there that you were getting soft.'

'Oh shut up, Harry,' she said. But she was smiling. 'I wonder how Michael and Angela are.' She shivered. 'I hope they're safe.'

*　★　*

'God bless them both,' said Anton, watching the screen as the train hit the water. The helicopter that was filming the scene swooped back, presumably to get to a safer distance. A few minutes later there was an enormous explosion, which carried sea water right up into the sky. It was close enough to splatter the windows of the palace, cracking some of them. Thankfully the damage was minimal and everyone inside the palace remained unharmed.

'Hopefully the worst that will happen to the remaining citizens is that they get wet,' said the Secretary of Defence.

'Nevertheless,' said Anton, 'contact emergency services and find out what help they may need. Also get a hazmat team in. We need to find out if we can lessen the effects of the radiation.'

'Anton,' said Faust, who was speaking on the telephone. 'I've just heard from the rescue people who have been working on the wreckage from the first carriages that came off. There are no casualties. In fact, there are no people.'

'That's something at least.'

'What about the other carriage?' asked Vicky.

'I was just getting to that,' said Faust. 'A few of them are injured but . . . '

'What?' she asked, her voice rising in panic. 'Tell me.'

'Solomon isn't among them. The young guard . . . the one called Will . . . said that Ambroise jumped off the train with Solomon in Austria. I'm afraid we don't know where he is, Miss Summers.'

Vicky put her face in her hands, and rubbed her eyes. 'He'll be alright,' she said. 'I know he will be. Ambroise will make sure he's safe.' She sounded as if she was trying to convince herself more than anything.

'I'm sure he will be,' said Anton. 'We'll send a search party to look for them in the region.'

'The problem,' said Faust, 'is that we don't know yet whose side Ambroise is on. He appeared to be working with the terrorists. I'm sorry, I don't want to dishearten you, but I don't think I should give you false hope either. Until Ambroise turns up with Solomon, we don't know what is going to happen.'

'Well,' said Alexander Summers, 'I hope now the danger is past, my daughter and I can leave.' He was sweating profusely and rubbing his head with a large white handkerchief.

'I'm staying here,' said Vicky. 'With His Majesty's permission.' Anton nodded his consent. 'I think Ambroise will bring Solomon here,' Vicky continued. 'Or, if Mr. di Luca is right about Ambroise being bad, he'll contact the palace with his demands.'

'Then I'll leave,' said Summers. 'I don't intend to stay here and be a martyr to someone else's cause.'

'We're talking about your grandson,' said Vicky, glaring at her father.

'There's one more thing,' said Faust, before Summers could reply. He and Anton exchanged glances. Anton nodded his agreement. At the same time, the two guards on the door stood to attention, blocking the doorway. 'Two more things actually. Do you want to tell him, Anton, or shall I?'

'Let me, please,' said Anton. 'We've been monitoring your calls since you arrived, Mr. Summers. We know you've been in contact with the train. We know you gave the order for Patty to shoot your son. And we know you and your backers are behind everything that's happened here today.'

'What?' Vicky looked at her father, more with resignation than with shock. 'You did all this? You put people's lives in danger so you could get the oil for your backers?'

'This is ridiculous,' Summers protested, but not very convincingly. 'Really, it's ludicrous. Come along, Vicky, I won't listen to another minute of this.' He moved to the door, only to find his way blocked by the guards.

'You said there were two things, Faust,' said Anton. 'I'm afraid I don't know what the second thing is. I assume it's more information that you've come across.'

'Yes,' said Faust, reaching into his pocket. He took out the fax that he had showed Vicky earlier. 'I think you should see this, Anton.'

'No!' Vicky exclaimed. 'Please, don't. I told you, I don't care.'

Anton took the fax. First of all he looked shocked, and then he looked relieved. 'I suppose that lets Miss Summers off the hook.'

'I'd say so.'

'What are you talking about?' asked Alexander Summers.

Anton held out the fax to him. Summers read it, and for the first time his arrogant stance failed him. His legs appeared to buckle. 'You little fool,' he said, turning on his daughter. 'If you'd told me earlier, none of this would have been necessary. Do you realise what you've done? You've almost got us both killed.'

He raised his hand, only to have Faust cross the room in an instant and grab his wrist. 'We don't hit women here, Mr. Summers.'

Summers appeared to regain control. He straightened up and brushed back his hair with one hand. 'Of course, this makes it all nice and legal. When my grandson is found, I trust you have no problems with him taking his rightful place as heir to Cariastan.'

'Over my dead body,' said Vicky. 'I don't want him to have that life. I want him to grow up as a normal little boy.'

'I'm afraid I don't understand,' said the Secretary of Defence. They had forgotten he was there. 'Your Majesty?'

'The fax,' Anton explained, 'is a copy of a marriage certificate. Miss Summers and my brother were married in Las Vegas. That means that young Solomon is the rightful heir to Cariastan.'

Summers grinned. 'And his grandfather will, of course, be there at his side.'

'No you won't,' said Vicky. 'You'll be in prison for terrorism.'

'I think you'll find I have much better backing than you can ever realise,' said Summers, sneering at his daughter and Anton. He took out his phone and started to make a call.

'Even if you wriggle your way out of this,' said Vicky, staying his hand. 'You're having nothing to do with my son. I will tell them to shoot you if you so much as come near to the palace.' She turned to Anton and Faust. 'You'll help me and Solomon, won't you? If my son really has to do this thing . . . if he's still alive . . . you'll help us?'

'Of course,' said Anton.

'Every step of the way,' said Faust. 'And if your father comes anywhere near, I'll shoot him myself.'

Vicky smiled shyly. 'Thank you . . . both.' But it seemed to everyone present that she was only speaking to Faust. 'Because I see now that the only way I'm going to keep him safe is to let him take his place in the palace. Not that I'm trying to usurp you.' That time she was talking to Anton. 'We don't have to tell anyone the truth.'

'I'm sure your father will,' said Anton. 'Whether he is in prison or not.'

Alexander Summers grinned. 'Oh yes. I'll make sure everyone knows. That child might as well have a target on his head.'

At that, Vicky reached up and punched her father in the nose, knocking him onto his back.

Summers jumped to his feet and pulled a gun from his coat pocket, aiming it at his daughter. 'How dare you? Do you realise the amount of planning that went into today? And all for you to blow the whole damn thing apart by coming here. We could have been out of the country by now, but oh no. You'd rather stay here and wait for the kid.' Summers cocked the gun. 'My children have been such a disappointment to me.'

'Put the gun down,' said Faust, who was standing next to one of the guards. Faust grabbed the guard's gun and pointed it at Summers. He could not get a good angle on Summers' head, and he did not want to shoot Vicky, but he was determined not to let that evil man walk away and benefit from his crimes.

'Don't be a fool, Summers,' said Anton. The tension in the room was electric.

'Don't tell me what to do, Your Royal Highness,' Summer sneered. 'You have no idea who is backing me. I've got the CIA in my pocket, and half a dozen other major players. By tomorrow I'll be living in a gated community in America, all paid for by the presidents of all the countries who want your oil. Because that's the only thing here worth having.'

There was an audible and collective gasp when Summers grabbed Vicky and pulled her in front of him, moving back towards the door, using her as a human shield. 'No one cares about the people in this stupid little country,' he hissed.

As he spoke, Vicky suddenly bent forward and used her elbows to hit her father in the stomach, winding him.

It gave Faust the clear target he needed. 'I care,' he said, pulling the trigger. Summers' head exploded and he slammed back against the door, landing in a crumpled heap.

Vicky looked at her father's prostrate body in horror and then ran into Faust's open arms.

★   ★   ★

Angela had dragged Mike up onto a sandy beach about half a mile away from where the train had crashed into the water. In the water, he had been light enough to pull along, but on the sand he was heavier. Still, she pulled him further inland. By that time, the bomb had not yet detonated, and she prided herself on how quickly she had moved him. But the further away they were from the explosion, the better.

She had managed to get him halfway up the beach when the bomb went off, soaking them both with an enormous wave of water. She covered his body with hers, as he coughed and spluttered beneath her. The water fell like a hundred knives onto her back, but at that moment she did not care. They were still alive. She would worry about the damage later.

The explosion subsided, taking the wave of water back with it. Finally they could breathe easily, though Angela was acutely aware that there may be radiation in the air. It made her want to hold her breath, but the innate fight for survival won out and she was soon breathing normally.

'I told you that you needed me with you,' she said to Mike, as he turned over to face her.

He stroked her wet hair. 'Yes you did, didn't you? I'd never have made it out of there if not for you.' He laughed. 'You mad, mad woman.'

'Of course you realise we're probably going to die from cancer now.'

'Always look on the bright side of life, eh?' Mike laughed again, but he was clearly in pain from the effects of the explosion, as she was.

Angela hoped that neither of them had suffered any internal damage. The way her ribs felt, it was possible that she had broken a couple. 'If you're going to start quoting Monty Python,' she said, 'I might just throw you back into the water. Mind you, you're the best looking fish I've ever caught.'

'You're the prettiest angler I've ever seen.'

'It's all quite biblical really, isn't it?' she said. 'Me, a vicar, water, fish.'

'That's probably blasphemous.'

As soon as Angela realised Mike was joking, she was going to kiss him. Suddenly the night sky above them became flooded with blue flashing lights. She waved the emergency services away. 'It's alright,' she said as medics ran towards them. 'We don't really need you lot anymore. We've saved the world without you.'

Nevertheless, within minutes they were surrounded, and bundled into an army ambulance.

★　★　★

'This is a really posh hospital,' said Angela, as she and Mike lay in adjoining beds in a room decorated with flocked wallpaper. The beds, though hospital beds, were soft and comfortable.

It was early morning, and they could see the sun rising outside the open drapes. The events of the night before seemed a long way away. They were not as badly injured as Angela had feared. None of their bones were broken, though Angela's ribs were badly bruised, and her back was very sore from where the water rained down on it. Mike still had a slight gunshot wound from the day before, but otherwise he was in good condition. Both were exhausted, and had been ordered to rest, but that was only to be expected.

'It's not a hospital,' said a good-looking man entering the small ward. 'Not a public hospital anyway. It's the medical wing of the palace. Hello, Reverend Fairfax, Miss Cunningham. I'm King Henri of Cariastan. Or at least I was. I suppose I can go back to being Anton now.' He took both their hands and shook them warmly, without explaining what he had just said. 'I can't even begin to repay you for the debt my country owes to you both.'

'I'm glad we could help,' said Mike.

'Me too,' said Angela. 'Have you heard from Ambroise and Solomon? Are they alright?'

'No news yet. Solomon's mother would like to talk to you in a short while, when you're feeling better. She just wants to know if her son was well treated by those who took him from her. Can I ask that you lie if you have to, to spare her feelings?'

'Yes, but you don't need to,' she replied. 'He wasn't treated warmly by Patty but I never saw her harm him. And I think Ambroise made up for it with the little lad.'

'Yes,' Mike agreed. 'He did his best to comfort the child.'

'You think Ambroise was on the side of the angels then?' asked Anton.

'I took that chance when I let him leave the train with Solomon,' said Angela. 'I pray that I was right.'

Anton nodded thoughtfully. 'Whatever happened after they left, I think that in that moment you saved the child's life. Alexander Summers proved himself to be ruthless. I have no doubt he would have tracked Ambroise and his grandson down and used the child again.'

'Is he under arrest?' asked Angela.

'No, he's dead.'

'Well, that's something,' said Angela. It seemed wrong to be glad of someone's death, but Summers had done more than most to earn it.

'Yes, although his part in all this is already being hushed up,' said Anton. 'We can't afford to expose the countries and agencies that had designs on our country. We're not strong enough. But it turns out that Summers had his fingers in lots of little pies too. He owned the security company, Belladonna, which trained female assassins like Patty, the woman on the train. We've been able to dismantle the company, but again Summers covered his tracks well, hiding behind lots of different corporations. The story is already going out that he lost his life helping people flee Cariastan. Only we know the truth.'

'What it is to be rich and powerful,' said Mike, with a steely note in his voice.

'And to have equally powerful friends,' said Anton. 'Anyway, now is not the time for regretting Mr. Summers' death or escape from censure. Now is the time to celebrate that Cariastan, thanks to you two, has averted a major catastrophe.'

'What about the radiation?' asked Angela.

'Ah, yes, I forgot to mention that,' said Anton. 'There isn't any.'

'What?' Mike and Angela said together.

'We've had people out all night checking for radiation and there isn't any, either in the sea or on the air. We think now that the bomb was a mock-up of a dirty bomb, made merely to spread fear and disruption and to try and force me off the throne. It makes sense, when you think about it. Summers and his people wanted the oil that has recently been found. If they had turned Cariastan into a radioactive wasteland, then it would have been a no-go area, even for them. It was mostly smoke and mirrors in the end.'

While Angela and Mike were digesting that information there was a gentle knock at the ward door. A pretty young fair-haired woman entered.

'You're Solomon's mum,' said Angela, with a warm smile. 'He has your eyes.'

Anton introduced Vicky Summers officially. 'Was he well when you last saw him?' Vicky asked eagerly, sitting on the edge of Angela's bed. Over a day of worrying was writ large in the poor girl's face.

'Yes, he was well and hadn't been mistreated as far as I could see. I think . . . ' Angela paused, not sure how much to say. 'I think they had sedated him once or twice, but that's all. I don't think it will have any lasting effects.'

'Except we don't know where he is,' said Vicky, looking crestfallen. Angela took her hand, wishing she could offer some comfort and encouragement. She had no idea if Ambroise and Solomon had made it safely off the train either and there was no sign of them yet. Despite saying she would lie, she felt it would be wrong to build up Vicky Summers' hopes.

'And my brother is under arrest,'

Vicky continued. 'Meanwhile my father is dead, so won't be brought to book for what he did. I hate that man,' she said, passionately. 'I always knew my father was cruel, but I never realised just how vicious he was until yesterday. I am so sorry for what he did.' She spoke not only to Angela and Mike, but also to Anton.

'It's not your fault,' said Angela, kindly.

Several hours later, Angela and Mike were both up and about, so Anton insisted that they have lunch with him. They were treated as honoured guests in the palace, and someone, Angela did not know who, had provided them with brand new clothes to wear. That the clothes were in the right sizes suggested that the palace was very well organised indeed. Everything was handled with quietness and dignity.

Before lunch, Angela could not resist taking a tour of the palace. She was accompanied by a guard, but otherwise allowed to go wherever she wanted. It was the most beautiful building she had ever seen, full of cool marble hallways, and a library that rivalled the Beast's in *Beauty and the Beast*. She thought that it might be nice to dance in there with Mike, but he had not chosen to do the tour, and she began to fear he was fed up of being around her. Telling herself she was being unfair, considering he was very tired and needed to rest, she pushed the thought aside.

At lunch they met Anton's friend, Faust di Luca. Angela idly wondered if ugly men were against the law in Cariastan. Every man she met, even the Secretary of Defence, was gorgeous. But she only had eyes for one man, and that was Mike. As far as she was concerned, he outshone them all. She felt a slight pang, knowing that their adventure was coming to a close, and that it would probably herald the end of whatever had bound them together for the past couple of days.

Vicky Summers ate with them, though it was noticeable that she only picked at her food. Her situation in the palace was explained to Angela and Mike, who, on learning all about Solomon's father, both felt as though a missing piece of a puzzle had slotted into place.

Every time a telephone rang in the palace, Vicky was on her feet, wondering if there was news of Solomon. When she was not doing that, she had Angela and Mike go over everything they knew about her son's time on the train. Every word he had said, and every time he might not have looked happy.

'I don't think he understood a lot of what was happening,' Angela said. 'To him it probably all seemed like an adventure. He was very good humoured through it all, though a little tired. That's understandable given the length of the trip.'

It was Faust di Luca's phone which rang rather than the main telephone. A big smile spread across his face. 'In that case,' he said, 'send them up immediately.'

'What is it?' asked Vicky.

'You'll see,' said Faust.

'Tell me.'

Everyone stood up and waited. Angela put her hand in Mike's, praying that Faust's smile had meant something good.

The door to the dining room opened, and a guard stepped in. Angela craned her neck to see behind him. As the guard moved out of the way, Ambroise came into view.

'Your Majesty,' he said, bowing to Anton. 'I'm sorry it took me so long to get here, but I felt it was best not to let anyone know of the precious burden I carried from Austria.' His one arm was in a sling. But cradled in his other arm was a sleeping child.

Vicky cried out and moved forward. As she did so, her son woke up and his face broke into a huge smile. 'Mamma,' he said, holding out his pudgy hands.

Vicky grabbed him and kissed his little face over and over again, with tears running down her cheeks. 'Thank you,' she said to Ambroise, reaching out and taking his good hand warmly. 'Thank you.'

'Thank God,' said Anton. 'Hello, Solomon,' he said, moving forward. 'You don't know me, but I'm your Uncle Anton.'

Solomon gave his new-found uncle a shy smile, but only had eyes for his mother. Ambroise, who looked as if he had been running on all his reserves, collapsed into a seat, but tried to stand again, as if afraid he was breaking protocol.

'I think you've earned a sit down,' said Anton.

Angela bit her lip, as the tears she had been holding back for so long threatened to fall. She looked across at Mike, who was smiling at Vicky and Solomon. It was all over. They were all safe at last. She should be happy for everyone.

Yet she also felt as if an important part of her life had come to an end.

15

The coronation of King Henri III was a very short affair, mainly on account of the new king needing to go and have his afternoon nap. Neither was he bothered about the champagne reception that took place afterwards. He left the party cradled in his proud mother's arms, whilst his doting uncle, the Lord Protector, Prince Anton, looked on with a contented smile on his face.

'I'm glad she's decided to accept your help,' Angela said to Anton. 'Life would have been very tough for her after what her father did.'

'Yes, we need to keep the little one safe,' said Anton. 'We can do that better here. I thank you both again for your help in bringing him to us.' He bowed courteously and left Angela and Mike standing together while he went to speak to a member of the British

Royal family who had come for the ceremony.

It had been a month since the explosive train journey that brought Angela and Mike hurtling into Cariastan. Most of that time had been taken up with being debriefed by the various international organisations who wanted to know exactly what had taken place. They had been followed by the world's media, who also wanted to know everything. In many ways it was more gruelling than being on the train. Angela wanted to run away and hide, but with the eyes of the entire world on her, and the other passengers, that was impossible. Another drawback was that she and Mike had barely had any time to talk to each other.

They stood together at the reception, both unsure what to say. The incident that had united them seemed like a dream. Angela feared that ordinary life would tear them apart.

'Oh there's Ambroise,' said Angela, waving to their new-found friend, and relieved to have someone else to speak to.

Ambroise came over to join them. He too looked very proud. 'It was a wonderful ceremony, was it not?' he asked.

'Yes it was,' said Mike. 'Short too. That's always a plus.'

Ambroise laughed. 'Yes, we feared His little Majesty may get a little fractious if we let things go on too long.'

'How are you?' asked Angela. 'Is your arm better?'

'Yes, thank you, Miss Cunningham.' Ambroise raised the arm, which was in a cast. 'The doctor says this can come off in a week or two.'

'I hope you don't mind me asking,' said Angela. 'But we've hardly had time to talk since everything happened. What were you doing on the train in the first place?'

'I have friends in low places,' said Ambroise. 'It sometimes helps to know such people when you work in security.

I heard rumours about what might happen, so I took a job on the train to keep an eye out. Unfortunately the terrorists were on to me very quickly. I presume they had checked on everyone who knew young Prince Solomon. Sorry, I should call him King Henri now. So I played the doting godfather instead and let them blackmail me into helping them with their scheme. I swear that even then I had no idea about the bomb. All I cared about was staying with the young prince until I could find a way to get him off the train. You helped me with that, Miss Cunning-ham, and I am grateful to you for trusting me.'

'I must admit I had my doubts for a while,' said Angela. 'I apologise for that.'

'There is no need for an apology. No one knew who to trust in that situation. Then we had to hide from Karloff and his men, who as you know, jumped off the train afterwards. We were in open country so I could see them from where we were, and I was afraid they might see us. That is why I did not contact anyone and tell them I had the child. In case they sent them looking for us.'

'That was sensible,' said Angela.

'I am sorry, however, for the pain I caused to Miss Summers. If I could have prevented that, I would.'

As Ambroise finished speaking, Will and Jon Bliss walked across to them. 'Hello, Monsieur Ambroise,' said Will. 'It sounds like you've had quite an adventure.'

'Ah, young Will,' said Ambroise. 'I owe you an apology. I have not been very kind to you in the past. I hope you will forgive me. I was under a lot of pressure, but I apologise for my behaviour.' He held out his good hand, which Will took with a big smile on his face.

'No problem, Monsieur. It was a heck of a journey.'

'Yes, indeed,' Ambroise agreed. 'Now, if you will excuse me, I will go and check on my young charge. He likes me to tell him a story before his nap.'

Angela and Will hugged, whilst Mike and Jon shook hands. Then they swapped. 'Write and let me know how you get on,' Angela said to Will.

'Of course,' said Will.'

'He's coming on tour with me,' said Jon. 'Then he's going to university. It's great, because I can help him now.'

'I told you that didn't matter,' said Will.

'Yeah, well I've got eighteen years of maintenance to make up for.'

They all stood chatting for a while, cheerfully discussing a future that a month before they feared they would never know.

'I'm so glad they were able to meet,' said Angela, when Will and Jon had gone off, talking about sightseeing in Cariastan. 'They're lucky they have each other to share this experience with.' She wondered how she would feel when she went home alone and had to live with the memories every day.

'Solomon is a lucky little boy too,'

said Mike. 'He's got two good father figures in his life. Prince Anton and Ambroise.'

'Three,' Angela corrected him.

'Three? Who's the other one?'

'The sexy one, Faust di Luca.'

'You think he's sexy?'

'Hell, yes. I think Vicky feels the same.'

'It doesn't seem to me that she likes him very much.'

'Oh that's because you're a man, Mike. You don't understand these things like women do.'

'I see. Well, if my radar is so broken I suppose I'm wasting my time here.'

'What do you mean?'

'Let's get out of here,' said Mike, taking Angela's champagne glass from her. He put their glasses on a side table, and took her hand. 'In many ways I envy young Solomon, being able to leave for a nap. I've certainly had enough pomp and circumstance for one day.'

They left the palace and walked to

the promenade in silence. It was a gloriously sunny day, and everything in Cariastan looked shining and bright. The people they passed smiled a welcome at them. Across the golden sands, the azure sea shimmered in the afternoon sunlight. 'It really is a beautiful little country,' said Angela. 'And the people are just lovely. It's a pity we haven't had chance to see more, what with the CIA and whatnot putting the thumbscrews on.'

'Yes, they were particularly interested, weren't they?' said Mike.

'They probably want to learn from their mistakes,' Angela mused. 'Oh, did I just say that out loud?'

'Yes, you did, and they've probably got a listening device trained on us,' said Mike, grinning. 'They won't be so gentle with us next time if they think we're on to them.'

'Hmm,' said Angela, pursing her lips.

They left the promenade, and went onto the beach. 'That was where we fetched up when the train crashed,' she said, pointing to a spot a little further along the beach.

'How is your back now? Is it still sore?'

'No, it's fine. Are you okay?'

'Yes, I'm fine.'

'Well, we're both fine then.'

Angela wondered why they seemed to have lost the easy chatter that they had shared when they first met. They had even joked about getting married. Now they could barely speak to each other, except for inane small talk. She wondered if Mike was feeling awkward about his offer. She really ought to say something.

'Mike?'

'Yes?'

'All that stuff on the train that we said . . . well, it was just the stress talking, wasn't it?'

'Was it?'

'Yes, of course. What I mean is that I don't . . . I won't hold you to any of it, if you're afraid that I might. We barely know each other, and everything that happened was a result of the tension we were under. It would be ludicrous for us to fall in love within twenty-four hours.'

'Oh yes, quite ludicrous,' said Mike.

Angela felt as though she had been punched in the heart. 'Yes, stupid,' she agreed, sadly.

'Because . . . ' Mike stopped on the sand overlooking the sea, and then turned Angela to face him. 'It took me a lot less time than that to fall in love with you.'

'Really?'

'Yes. In fact, I'd say it was . . . oh, at least twenty-four minutes before I realised I didn't want to spend the rest of my life without you.'

'Twenty-four whole minutes?' Angela smiled ecstatically. 'Why?' she teased. 'What was wrong with me for the first twenty-three minutes?'

'You were trying to make me sleep in the restaurant car, whilst you had the nice comfortable bunk.'

'That was only because I didn't trust

myself not to ravage you.'

Mike answered her with a kiss that made the sun shine brighter and the sea turn bluer. 'Ravage away,' he said, when he had finished kissing her.

'You're a vicar. You really shouldn't say such things.'

'I'm a man first. You might have thought I was joking about marrying you, but I wasn't. My darling . . . ' He held her closer. 'I thought that when I lost Julia I'd been lucky enough to love and be loved once in my lifetime. I didn't expect it ever to happen again. But I do love you, and I hope you love me.'

'I love you desperately, Mike. However, I do want to state for the record that it only took me about twenty-four seconds to fall in love with you.'

'Why? What was wrong with me for the first twenty-three seconds?'

'You had your back to me.'

Mike laughed and lifted her into the air, spinning her around. 'Will you marry me?'

'Oh yes!'

'Shall we go on a train trip for our honeymoon?' he asked with a wink.

'I'm never setting foot on a train again. Let's go by boat instead.'

'I can't swim. Remember?'

'But you'll have me to save you.'

He stroked her cheek. 'You have saved me, Angela Cunningham. More than you can ever know.'

THE END

We do hope that you have enjoyed reading this large print book.

Did you know that all of our titles are available for purchase?

We publish a wide range of high quality large print books including:
Romances, Mysteries, Classics
General Fiction
Non Fiction and Westerns

Special interest titles available in large print are:
The Little Oxford Dictionary
Music Book, Song Book
Hymn Book, Service Book

Also available from us courtesy of Oxford University Press:
Young Readers' Dictionary
(large print edition)
Young Readers' Thesaurus
(large print edition)

For further information or a free brochure, please contact us at:
Ulverscroft Large Print Books Ltd.,
The Green, Bradgate Road, Anstey,
Leicester, LE7 7FU, England.
Tel: (00 44) **0116 236 4325**
Fax: (00 44) **0116 234 0205**

Other titles in the
Linford Romance Library:

SURGEON IN PORTUGAL

Anna Ramsay

'A strong dose of sunshine' is the prescription for Nurse Liz Larking, recovering from glandular fever. And a villa in the Algarve seems the ideal place to recuperate, even if it means cooking for the villa's owner, eminent cardiac surgeon Hugh Forsythe: brilliant, caring, awe-inspiring — and dangerously easy to fall in love with. Liz soon realises that this doctor is more potent than any virus — and ironically, it seems he could just as easily break a heart as cure one . . .

CINDERELLA SRN

Anna Ramsay

Despite her tender years, Student Nurse Kate Cameron is like a mother hen, forever worrying about her patients and her family. So it's a huge joke when her friends transform her into a *femme fatale* for the hospital's Christmas Ball. The joke backfires though, when Kate finds herself falling in love . . . But what chance is there of a fairy-tale ending when this Cinderella has chapped hands and an unflattering uniform, and Prince Charming turns out to be Luke Harvey, the new senior registrar?

A VERY SPECIAL GIRL

Renee Shann

Though warned by her parents, Emma marries Nicholas Stagger, a Krasnovian from Traj. Too late she has found that her parents were right, for Nicky's infidelities are more than she can stand. Furthermore, Nicky's involvement in the politics of his own country brings Emma herself into danger; but it is through this involvement that she meets Paul, President of Krasnovia. At last Emma can see her future clearly, but danger still awaits . . .

NORTH BY NORTHEAST

Phyllis Humphrey

Haley Parsons, a school teacher on her first real vacation in years, boards the beautiful and luxurious American Orient Express for a week-long train excursion from New Orleans to Washington, D.C. . But then her jewelry begins to disappear and she finds herself an unwitting player in a kidnapping and robbery attempt. The culprit is evidently aboard the train; and Jonathan Shafer, Haley's handsome, new-found love interest, is somehow involved. Who is he, really? And what part will he play in all this?

A TEMPORARY LOVER

Carol Wood

Sophie Shaw had taken pride and pleasure in building up a veterinary practice with her husband Michael and his partner, but Michael's death had left a void in her life. It seemed none of the applicants for the practice was right — until Luke Jordon pointed out that *she* was the problem. Once Luke began his duties, Sophie had to admit that he was an excellent vet, but he also raised a frisson in her that had nothing to do with work . . .

FROM FAR AWAY

Dorothy Black

It is unusual to see a visitor in the fells in the depths of winter. 'What would bring Leonie Elwood, society beauty and adored child of a millionaire, to the desolate moors on such a day?' wonders the old woman who opens the door and gives her sanctuary, though her heart warns her of the consequences. For Leonie soon loses her heart to Martin Langley, whose mother protects him with the ferocity of a tigress . . .